Sealed With a Kiss

Books by Beverly Lewis

GIRLS ONLY (GO!)
Youth Fiction

Dreams on Ice	*Follow the Dream*
Only the Best	*Better Than Best*
A Perfect Match	*Photo Perfect*
Reach for the Stars	*Star Status*

SUMMERHILL SECRETS
Youth Fiction

Whispers Down the Lane	*House of Secrets*
Secret in the Willows	*Echoes in the Wind*
Catch a Falling Star	*Hide Behind the Moon*
Night of the Fireflies	*Windows on the Hill*
A Cry in the Dark	*Shadows Beyond the Gate*

HOLLY'S HEART
Youth Fiction

Best Friend, Worst Enemy	*Straight-A Teacher*
Secret Summer Dreams	*No Guys Pact*
Sealed With a Kiss	*Little White Lies*
The Trouble With Weddings	*Freshman Frenzy*
California Crazy	*Mystery Letters*
Second-Best Friend	*Eight Is Enough*
Good-Bye, Dressel Hills	*It's a Girl Thing*

www.BeverlyLewis.com

Holly's Heart

Sealed With
a Kiss

Beverly Lewis

BETHANYHOUSE
Minneapolis, Minnesota

Sealed With a Kiss
Revised edition 2002
Copyright © 1993, 2002
Beverly Lewis

Cover illustration by Paul Casale
Cover design by Cheryl Neisen

Published by Bethany House Publishers
11400 Hampshire Avenue South
Bloomington, Minnesota 55438

Bethany House Publishers is a division of
Baker Publishing Group, Grand Rapids, Michigan.

Printed in the United States of America

Library of Congress Cataloging-in-Publication Data

Lewis, Beverly, 1949-
   Sealed with a kiss / by Beverly Lewis.
       p.   cm. — (Holly's heart ; 3)
Summary: While competing with her friend Andie to see who can collect the most pen pals, Holly commits an act of dishonesty by misrepresenting herself to her newest correspondent.
   ISBN 0-7642-2502-2
   [1. Pen pals—Fiction. 2. Honesty—Fiction.] I. Title.
PZ7.L58464 SD   2002
   [Fic]—dc21   2001005679

Author's Note

Hugs to my fabulous teen consultants and reviewers.

Hurrah for my SCBWI critique group, who offered valuable assistance on the manuscript, as well as Barbara Birch and my husband, Dave.

Applause to my editor, Rochelle Glöege, for her thoughtful suggestions and expert help.

Thanks to Del Gariepy, who helped with medical questions.

To

Julie Marie,

my number one fad 'n' fashion expert,

and a "hearts-and-flowers" girl.

1

"Holly!" called my best friend, Andrea Martinez. "Come up here."

"No way," I said. "I don't want to fall into the Arkansas River!" I plunged my paddle into the frothing white water for stability, holding it like the balancing pole of a high-wire acrobat.

"Aw, don't be such a scaredy," Andie hollered back. "Shooting the rapids up here is the only way to go!" She was sitting on the bow of our raft, showing off for Billy Hill, who worked the paddles with Danny Myers and Andie's dad. She put down her paddle and held up her hands. "Look, no hands!" she squealed as Billy, her current heart-throb, grinned.

"You've gotta be crazy," I said, watching the boulders coming up on the left.

Danny shook his head, obviously disgusted with her antics. He relaxed his grip on the paddles as we floated into calmer water.

River rafting on the mighty Arkansas was the most excitement I'd had all summer, not counting the weeks I'd spent with my dad in California two months ago.

"Hold on now, Andie," her father warned. "The current's picking up." A river runner from back in his college days, Mr. Martinez knew this river. But that was twenty years ago. Now he was our paddle captain.

Brett, the *real* pro, our guide, sat next to Andie's dad. He was blond and tan, probably from a Colorado summer of river trips.

If Danny hadn't been paddling next to me in the raft, I might have been tempted to ask Brett for a crash course in white-water rafting. Not that Danny wasn't as good-looking. He was! He had thick, auburnish brown hair, and eyes a toss-up between gray and green, depending on the color of his shirt. But Brett had that smooth, collegiate look.

Stealing another glance at Brett, I figured he was probably halfway through college. But most sophisticated older guys don't usually go for eighth-grade girls. So much for my silly microfantasy.

Danny turned to see how I was doing on my first river ride. With Billy and Andie along, the adventure was almost like a double date, except for Andie's parents and Brett, who wore a look of mature confidence. I still could hardly believe Andie and I had pulled it off, talking our parents into allowing Danny and Billy to come along.

Entering a wild stretch of river, the guys strained to control the paddles. I managed to steady mine. So far, it wasn't too hard, only because the real work was being accomplished by the others.

Andie took the big waves with ease as she rode up front, grinning from ear to ear. "C'mon, Holly," she called again. "You should try it up here. The view's great."

"No, thanks." A spray of water made me jump. "I'd like

to live long enough to become a published writer."

Andie just laughed.

The rapids came every half mile or so, like clockwork. And on cue—in the middle of the churning white water—Andie hammed it up. Probably for Billy's sake and anyone else who might pay attention.

After the white water, we drifted downstream as gentle breezes cooled my sunburned face. Andie's mom chatted with Billy. Now and then she called up to Andie in front. "Hanging on, kiddo?"

Andie tightened her life vest at the waist. "I'm fine, Mom, see?"

Billy told Andie, "White-water rafting isn't dangerous unless you're careless." Pretending to be serious, he said, "So you'd better watch out." Then he laughed.

"This is only your first run down a river, Billy," Andie teased. "What are *you* talking about?"

Danny was more sincere. "There's a certain amount of respect you show a river as powerful as the Arkansas."

Andie rolled her eyes at that statement and continued to banter back and forth with Billy as we drifted lazily in the warm sunshine. Giant granite walls towered on either side of us, and huge boulders dotted the banks.

Andie's dad didn't seem worried about his daughter clowning around, so I tried to relax about it, talking quietly to Danny. Sounds carry on the river like an amplifier. We could hear voices from another outfitter upstream, so I turned *my* volume down.

I liked Danny. Being here on a twelve-mile raft trip with him in the middle of Browns Canyon, hours from home, was so special. It was like hanging out in our own corner of the world.

With Danny right in front of me, I felt safe, the way I'd felt when I visited Daddy in California. But I couldn't second-guess Danny; even though he was attentive enough, I really didn't know how he felt about me.

Brett shouted back to us, "Hang on. Turbulent waters coming!"

Up ahead, I spotted some boulders in midstream. Excited, I asked, "Is this the Widowmaker?"

"The river map indicates it," Danny answered. With his photographic memory, he never forgot anything.

Peering around Danny, I could see sprays of white water about fifty yards ahead. My five-foot paddle suddenly felt heavy as I gripped it. The Widowmaker!

Water swirled around us like a milky-white hurricane. I felt dizzy staring into the frothing waters. I heard its roar as I paddled with decisive strokes. My adrenaline pumped as a giddy yet courageous feeling struck me.

As we dodged the boulders, I could see the cliffs getting closer.

I swallowed nervously, my arms aching as we fought to get out of the current. The raft climbed a current, then fell, spraying us with icy water. Wiping my face with my arm, I paddled harder than ever.

Just when we cut into the water and were winning the race against the river's current, Andie lurched off balance. Her hands slipped away from the raft as she screamed. And then she flipped out of the raft into the swirling, icy waters.

"Andie . . . no!" I cried, lunging toward her, falling against Danny.

But she was gone. Lost in the rapids!

2

Andie's dad instantly dove into the river. All of us watched in horror as he tried to swim toward Andie, the current tossing him like a pebble.

Andie's mom was shouting, "Brett, please get them! Help them!"

His face tense, Brett steadied the paddles, fighting the current. He called to Andie's father, "Grab her and ride it out."

Mr. Martinez reached toward his daughter as another series of waves pushed Andie away, below the surface. My best friend in the whole world had disappeared from view.

Seconds passed as I held my breath. Still no Andie. *Let her be safe. Please, Lord, don't let her die!*

Another second or two ticked by. Then I saw her dark curly hair, and her arms smashing against the current.

"There she is!" I yelled as her father fired forward, grabbing her right arm in his fist.

The two of them bobbed in the current, narrowly missing the rocks. Soon the rapids became less violent, and Brett tossed out a long line with a throw bag at the end.

Andie's dad grabbed for the white bag at the end of the nylon rope.

My heart pounded a zillion miles an hour. Feeling helpless, I started to cry.

Danny touched my hand. "They're gonna make it, Holly," he said.

"Row to the right," Brett shouted to us. We paddled toward an eddy along the bank to keep from being swept farther downstream. Brett shortened the line, and the current made it taut. Straining through the bleak waters, grasping the line, Andie and her father inched closer . . . closer. Then they were close enough to reach out and grab the sides of the raft.

"I'm fr-freezing," Andie chattered as Billy pulled her limp body on board. Her father slid into the raft, bringing gallons of the river with him.

"Let's paddle to shore," Brett ordered.

We made a quick landfall, and Brett began pulling a pile of wool blankets out of the narrow waterproof box secured to the bottom of the raft. "Hurry! Get her out of those wet clothes and wrap her in these." He handed the blankets to Andie's mom. "Every second counts. We must get her body temperature back to normal." Then he turned to Danny and Billy. "You guys scrounge up some dry firewood. I'll check on Andie's dad."

Brett, carrying a small paramedic's bag and a blanket, raced over to Mr. Martinez. He was sitting on the ground, vigorously rubbing his arms and legs.

I followed Andie and her mom a few yards away, where I held up one of the wool blankets for privacy. By now Andie was shivering so hard she could scarcely talk. Her mother pulled off the wet outer clothes. I was poised for action, with the wool blanket ready to wrap around Andie.

I noticed the strange look in her eyes, like she wasn't focusing. Her mom must've seen how scared I was. "This is hypothermia," she said calmly. But her hands shook as she helped Andie dry off. We wrapped another blanket around Andie's body and led her to a crackling fire, where Brett was heating water for a hot drink.

Andie's dad was more alert and active than Andie, slapping his arms and moving his feet to get the circulation going. Maybe the weight of his body had given him some insulation against the icy water. But it was obvious they'd both had a thrashing.

Andie slumped to the ground near the fire, shivering. I stared at my friend, who looked like a half-drowned river rat, her lips colorless, her teeth chattering. She was almost too weak to sit up.

Hurrying to her side, I sat cross-legged on the ground. I leaned against her, rubbing her back to help the circulation. Her mom snuggled against her on the other side.

"You're going to be okay," I said, trying to convince myself as well as Andie.

She only nodded. It wasn't like her to be so quiet. She was usually a chatterbox. In fact, she'd talked me into being her best friend before I even had a chance to think about it! We'd laughed our way through grade school together, spent fabulous camping vacations together, and even survived seventh grade last school year. Together. She was my complete opposite: the chattery, uninhibited half of us.

In spite of her feisty ways, Andie was my dearest friend. Seeing her nearly drown today had been the next-to-worst experience of my life. Mom and Daddy's divorce was the all-time worst, though.

I stared into the fire's tall blaze. Daddy had made a similar bonfire on the beach one night last June when I visited him. We'd talked about life and fear and other difficult things. Just the two of us.

Finally I got around to telling him about my faith in Christ. He didn't say much more after that. It was like my discussing it ruined the rest of the evening for him.

Just then Andie mumbled something, and her mom wrapped her arms around her shoulders.

Brett stirred powdered Jell-O into the hot water. "Here, this'll help warm her up." He handed the mug to Andie's mom, who held the mug to Andie's lips, helping her sip slowly.

I watched her face. She still seemed dazed. "Andie," I said, "your rescue has to be a sign from heaven."

"Heaven?" she whispered.

"God has something important for you to do here on earth." I'd always thought that way about successful rescue attempts. People didn't just get spared or get their lives back for no reason. At least not trivial ones. Surely God had Andie marked for some favored mission.

Billy burst into laughter. "Yeah, Andie, maybe you're supposed to try out for girls' volleyball after all."

I poked him in the ribs. "That's *not* what I meant."

Like some miracle, Andie snickered. "What Holly means is God has something more important planned for me than girls' volleyball," she said. "Besides, there's no way they'll want someone as short as I am on the team."

Brett flashed a smile our way. "Looks like she's coming around." He seemed relieved. So was I.

Danny slid a bit closer to me. "Why don't *you* try out for the team, Holly?"

I was dying to. "Perfect idea," I said. "Besides, I heard Miss Neff isn't coaching next year." The gym teacher with a knack for creating lousy nicknames had kept me from playing sports because of her nickname for me: *Holly-Bones.* Verbal disrespect for slender humanity!

"Miss Neff is a great coach. Don't you like her?" Danny asked.

Andie cast a knowing smile. "Miss Neff has a bad habit of teasing skinny girls."

"So who's skinny?" Billy joked, looking around.

Danny ignored him. "Too bad you didn't try out in seventh grade, Holly. You could've easily made the team last year," he said. "It might be hard to get on the B team now, without that year of experience."

"But if I practice after school, won't that help?"

Danny nodded. "Let me know when you want to practice. I could coach you, too."

Andie raised her eyebrows. "Who *else* is getting tips from the pro?"

"Just Kayla Miller," he said. "You remember her, don't you? She hopes to make the team, too. She played back east at her school in Pennsylvania, before moving to Dressel Hills."

"What about her twin sister?" Billy asked. "Are you going to put *both* brunettes through their paces?"

"Last I heard, Jared Wilkins is helping Paula," Danny said.

Jared? Hearing his name still brought back sad memories. Guess a girl always remembers the first major crush of her life.

Having both Danny *and* Jared link up with the Miller twins made me nervous. Maybe Danny sensed my uneasiness, because at that moment he caught me by surprise. He turned toward me and touched my elbow. His gray-green eyes twinkled and my heart leaped up. Thoughts of Jared Wilkins floated far away.

I smiled back, feeling the warmth in my cheeks. Was Danny's offer to help me make the volleyball team the beginning of a really close friendship? Or was it just another one of his big-brother routines?

3

My first volleyball practice session with Danny began two days after the raft trip. We started by working on my serve. A regulation-size net hung between two aspen trees in his backyard. After only two tries, I hit the ball over the net.

"You're a natural," Danny said. "Now let's try spiking the ball when the net's in your face."

We worked on techniques like how to get under the ball and how to spike. But just as Danny was about to demonstrate a new move, along came Billy Hill and half the church youth group. Well, actually it was only Andie, the Miller twins, and Jared Wilkins. Some private lesson this was turning out to be.

"Girls against the guys," called Andie.

Paula and Kayla Miller smiled, their perfect teeth glistening in the August sunshine.

"You're on," Jared said, spinning the volleyball on his pointer finger.

Danny's parents came outside and stood on the redwood deck. "Room for two more?" asked Danny's dad.

"C'mon down," said Billy, motioning to them.

The neighbors next door peered over the fence. Danny waved and *they* joined us, too.

Since the sides were uneven, Danny volunteered to referee. Paula Miller went over to play on the guys' side. She seemed flattered as Jared lifted the net when she ducked under. I wondered if she cared that Jared was the world's worst two-timer. Andie was watching Paula, too, as Jared turned on his charm. Too bad. Both Andie and I knew firsthand how it felt to be fooled by Jared.

Danny put his fingers between his teeth and whistled. "Ladies first," he said. Our side cheered its approval.

Andie served, and Billy bumped the ball back to our side. Kayla set me up, and I spiked it down right in front of Jared. He missed. Our first point.

"Check it out," called Andie. "Holly's volleys can't be beat." Everyone laughed except Paula's twin, Kayla, who seemed more interested in watching Danny. Lucky for me, he was too busy keeping score to notice.

A few minutes later it was my serve. I glanced at Danny anxiously. He encouraged me with his grin and a gesture, a reminder to get down under the ball and follow through with the forearm motion he'd shown me today . . . before the crowd showed up.

I stepped back, took a deep breath, and served. The ball barely missed the net. Billy set it up for Danny's dad, who tapped it with his fingers. Jared came in for the kill.

I saw it coming and moved out of my position in the back row. Leaning down, I got under the ball. It shot high enough for Danny's mom to punch it over the net.

We volleyed back and forth three more times before Billy fumbled. Our score again!

For some reason, we were unbeatable. After winning

two games in a row, we broke for a snack of chips, dip, and pop.

Danny invited me up to the patio, where he introduced me to his parents.

"We've seen you singing in the youth choir at church," his dad said. "It's nice to meet you finally."

Finally? What did that mean?

Danny's mom was pleasant. "Please come over any time, Holly," she said. Her smile reminded me of Danny's. "We love to entertain our son's friends."

"Thanks, Mrs. Myers," I said politely, hoping we could get better acquainted soon. There was so much I didn't know about Danny.

He carried the bowls of chips around the yard, stopping to talk to Kayla longer than any of the other girls. Her brunette hair was pulled to the back of her head in a ponytail and secured with a red beaded twist. Paula was sitting with Jared in the far corner of the yard, under a stand of aspen trees. She wore her hair the same as Kayla, only it was secured with an orange twist.

Just then Andie came running. She grabbed my arm and asked Danny's mom where the bathroom was.

"Through these doors you'll see the powder room to the left of the kitchen," Mrs. Myers told her.

"Are you sick?" I asked Andie, locking the bathroom door behind us.

"No, but *you* might be when you hear this," she whispered. "Kayla likes Danny."

"I noticed," I said. "But worse—what if *he* likes *her*, too?"

"Danny's just exceptionally polite," Andie said. "That's all it is."

I noticed the luxurious apricot-colored towels nearby. There was crocheting on the edges and a monogrammed M on each one, even the washcloths.

"His parents must be rolling in it," I said.

Andie eyed the towels. "Give me a break. Nice towels don't mean anything."

Washing my hands in the cream-colored sink, I enjoyed the lilac potpourri in a small basket on the counter. "What if Kayla Miller and Danny have money in common?" I said. "What about that?"

"If you're going to freak out, just think about being stuck in eighth grade while Danny and Kayla trade notes in advanced math class, one grade higher."

I sighed. "You're right. They were in algebra together last semester, when the Millers moved here in April. Yikes."

Andie picked up the gold-plated soap dish. "Now *this* is expensive," she whispered. "Maybe you're right. Maybe Danny's folks are—"

"Who's in there?" cooed a female voice.

"Shouldn't you say 'knock, knock' first?" Andie asked.

"Okay. Knock, knock."

"Who's there?" we answered in unison.

"Justin."

"Justin who?" we asked, puzzled.

"Just in time for another game. Wanna play?"

I opened the door to see Kayla and Paula, the pony-tailed wonders.

Andie giggled. "Hey, you're good," she said. "You fooled us. We thought there was only *one* of you talking."

Heading toward the sliding glass door leading to the patio, I lagged behind. The draperies in the family room matched the print of the sofa. Shelves filled with books covered the far wall. And was that a crystal chandelier over the dining room table? Money! They had it, all right.

♥   ♥   ♥

We played volleyball until it got too dark to see, even with the impressive floodlights which came on automatically around the yard.

When it came time, Danny's father offered to drive Andie and me home. I jumped at the chance to ride in his new Lexus SUV. Unfortunately the Miller twins were also included in the invitation. So I had to share Danny. Again.

Paula and Kayla's house stood on the side of a hill in another classy part of town. As we turned into their steep driveway, Kayla asked Danny when they could get together to work on her serve. It wasn't what she said but *how* she said it that made me swallow to keep from choking. Talk about flirting. The girl had it down to an art form.

"What about tomorrow around three?" Danny's response was almost businesslike. But that was his way. He was probably totally in the dark about Kayla's cooing.

Tomorrow afternoon Danny and Kayla would practice volleyball techniques together. Unless I could spoil their plans somehow . . .

Danny's dad made small talk as he drove down the tree-lined streets toward Downhill Court. His sports utility vehicle was sleek and comfortable, and it made me think of one of my pen pals, Lucas Leigh. Recently, Lucas had written that he was car shopping. *I'm considering a Corvette, but there's nothing like a Porsche*, he'd written in his last letter.

I knew absolutely zip about sports cars, except that they were flashy and fast. As for me, this Lexus was cool potatoes!

When we arrived at my house, I thanked both Danny and his dad for a fabulous time. Then Andie and I scurried up the steps and into the house.

Goofey, my motley-colored cat, sat curled up under the card table. Mom and her date, Mr. Tate, were playing checkers in the living room.

"Hi, Mom," I said, kissing her cheek lightly.

Andie and I stood there for a moment, staring at the red kings invading Mom's territory. "Looks like you're surrounded," Andie said.

Mr. Tate looked up momentarily. "Holly," he said to me, "your mother saved leftovers for you and your friend."

"Thanks, Mom," I said softly. *To her.*

Mr. Tate continued to study me. "And," he said, pausing like what he was about to say was very important, "this is your night to clean up the kitchen."

Mom turned to me. "Because your sister's spending the night with Stephanie."

"Uncle Jack and my cousins arrived?" I said, thrilled to hear the news.

"Not Uncle Jack and the boys, just Stephanie," Mom explained. "She didn't want to go on a business trip with her dad, so she's staying at the Millers' house till Uncle Jack returns."

I glanced at Andie. "We were just at the Millers', dropping Paula and Kayla off."

"Well, that's where Stephanie's staying for now," Mom said, focusing on the game again.

"Why didn't *we* keep her?" I asked.

"Because I didn't want *you* to be stuck baby-sitting during your final days of summer vacation," Mom said. "Besides, Paula and Kayla baby-sat Stephie all the time when they lived in Pennsylvania."

The twins' father, Mr. Miller, had worked for the same company as Uncle Jack. After much persuading from the Millers, Uncle Jack decided to move to our ski village—Dressel Hills—after his wife, my dad's sister—aunt Marla—died last February.

"When is Uncle Jack actually coming to town?" I asked.

"Last I heard, in a few weeks." Mom's checker was close to being snatched by Mr. Tate's king.

Mom's date stared at me. "You have kitchen duty, Holly," the not-so-great Mr. Tate said. A control freak, he was growing worse by the week.

In the kitchen, Andie and I loaded the dishwasher. "So . . . has you-know-who rearranged your life yet?" She was wise to keep her voice low.

I snickered. "That's just how he is. Could be that he's the take-charge type because of Zachary's cancer. Speaking of which . . ."

"E-ee-ow, zoom, crash!" Here came Zach. He'd grown just a little over the summer, but for a nine-year-old, he was still very small.

"Hey, Zach. How're you doing?" I asked as he ka-boomed and gazoomed his fighter plane in right patterns around us.

"I'm remissed," he said.

"He's what?" Andie asked.

Zach jumped up and down, trying to get the word out. "I'm getting well. I'm remissed."

"That's great news," I said, giving him not-so-high fives all around the kitchen. "His cancer's in remission," I told Andie, who poured the powdered soap into the dishwasher.

"Let's celebrate," Zach said, opening the freezer and poking around, trying to find some strawberry ice cream.

"Hold on." I rushed back into the living room.

Mr. Tate looked up as I came in, the top of his bald head shiny with beads of perspiration. Seemed like he was playing checkers for keeps.

"That's fabulous news about Zachary," I said, thrilled.

"We're delighted, too." Mom clasped her hands together. "An answer to our prayers."

Mr. Tate's face broke into a rare smile. He reached for Mom's hand. "Now your mother and I can make the plans we had to put on hold for a few months."

Gulp!

Staring into this man's eyes, I was certain he wasn't the best replacement for Daddy. Could I live with him calling all the shots, stepping in all too eagerly as Mom's husband and my step . . . uh, father?

Zach was back in my face with a dipper for the ice cream.

"Is it okay with you?" I asked his dad.

Dramatically, Mr. Tate stretched his arm out to peer at his watch. "I believe it's too late for sweets," he announced.

"Aw, Dad," Zach whined.

Mom intervened. "But it's such a special time."

This was a mistake. By the look on Mr. Tate's face, Mom's pleading hadn't gone over too well. He simply shook his head with great finality.

Mom wilted.

Andie motioned to me from the doorway. *She* didn't

think it was too late for sweets. And I wasn't about to ask Mr. Tate's permission, either.

I joined her in the kitchen, where I spotted today's stack of mail on the desk. Sorting through it, I discovered a letter addressed to Mom. On the envelope, our address, *207 Downhill Court, Dressel Hills, Colorado*, was followed by a large *U.S.A.*

"Who's this from?" I muttered, showing Andie the stamp.

She rotated the envelope, studying the postmark. "It's from Japan. Does your mom have a pen pal there?"

"Let me see that." I held it up to the light. "It's hand-written." My curiosity grew as I glanced toward the checker game in the living room.

I got Zach's attention. "Do you know when you and your dad are heading home tonight?" I asked.

"Nope," he said, carrying his jet planes and gazoomer stuff down to the family room.

I whispered to Andie, "I hope they leave soon."

Sliding the mystery letter under the pile of mail, I dished up ice cream in record time. Andie and I smuggled our bowls upstairs. "Nothing like a huge bowl of strawberry ice cream shared with a best friend." I closed my bedroom door behind me.

Andie laughed. "Sounds like a verse on a greeting card."

"I'd rather write stories." I paused, thinking about that. "Or letters." Lucas Leigh, my secret pen pal, flashed across my thoughts.

"Do you think your mom will let you read her letter?" Andie asked, taking a giant bite of ice cream.

"Mom tells me everything," I said.

"Everything?"

"Well, close," I said, spooning up a tiny bite and relishing the fruity flavor.

"Think she'll marry Mr. Tate?" At that Andie stuck her nose in the air, imitating the man's response to Zach's request for ice cream.

"Not if I can help it," I said with more confidence than ever. "Now, we need to devise a plan to ruin Kayla's volleyball lesson with Danny tomorrow."

Andie leaned back on her elbow on the floor. "Your little sister is staying with Stephanie over at the Millers', right?"

I nodded.

A gleam of mischief twinkled in her brown eyes. "Can you arrange for her to stay there all afternoon?"

"Easy," I said. Andie was on to something and it was perfect. "Let's call Jared and tell him Paula's coming over *here* tomorrow at three."

A silly grin played across her face. "Great idea!"

"Wait," I said, reaching for the phone and handing it to Andie. "What if he can't come?"

"There's no way Jared would miss out on some female attention."

"Andie, you're a genius!"

"Put that in writing, would you?" She dialed the numbers for Jared's house. If this little scheme worked, Kayla would have to take Stephie and Carrie along when she practiced volleyball with Danny because her sister, Paula, would be busy, over here visiting me. Until Jared showed up, that is.

Giggling, I waited. "This is the Plan of the Hour," I whispered.

Andie shushed me. "C'mon, Jared, answer the phone." A few more seconds ticked by, then she gave up. "I'll call later."

I went to my window seat, facing Andie, who'd flopped down on the floor. "How long do we wait before we phone Jared again?"

"Five minutes," she said. "Maybe he's in the shower. . . . Can a guy take one that fast?"

"Maybe," I said, reaching for Bearie-O, my favorite teddy bear, who was really Andie's. We'd traded best bears back in first grade, almost half a lifetime ago.

"Well, I can't shower in five minutes. My hair's so thick it takes that long just to get the shampoo rinsed out."

"I know what you mean." I draped my hair over my arm. "This takes half a day to dry."

"Ever wish you could whack it off?"

I stared down at the blond strands. "Not really. Why?"

"Just wondered," Andie said, watching the minute hand on her watch. "You've never really cut it your whole life."

"It's probably the best part of me," I said.

"And boys like long hair," she said matter-of-factly.

"That's not all," I muttered. "They like girls with perfect shapes. Like the Miller twins."

"Don't forget personality. *You* have that. Besides, you're tall and slender and—"

"Make that *skinny* and underdeveloped," I interrupted. "People don't call me 'bones' for nothing."

"*People* don't. Miss Neff is just one person, and she probably calls you Holly-Bones because she thinks you can handle the teasing."

I sighed. "When school starts, I'll tell her I hate it. Then maybe she'll stop."

"You might not have a chance, you know. You're getting rounder and rounder—where it counts," she said in a silly voice. "Take it from your best friend, which is, by the way, another good thing you've got going for you."

I squeezed Bearie-O. "Why did Paula and Kayla Miller have to move here right when Danny and I were—"

"Holly!" Mom called from downstairs.

I took the steps down two at a time. "What is it, Mom?"

"That's what I'd like to know," she said, waving the mystery letter.

I scanned the living room for Mr. Tate. The house was empty. "Who's it from?"

"It's not signed," she said. "And no return address."

"What's it say?" By now Andie was at my side.

"It's very short, almost childish, but definitely humorous." Mom handed the letter to me.

I studied the handwriting on the envelope. The penmanship was scrawled. "Do you recognize the writing?"

Mom shook her head.

I opened the letter and read:

Dearest Susan,

I still remember the first time I saw you. It was a long time ago. I wish I could see you more often, the way it used to be. Please remember to laugh like in the old days. Okay?

Here's a joke to help you do that. Why doesn't a bald man need any keys? Because he has no locks. Ha, ha. (No offense.)

I miss you. I'll write again. Maybe sooner than you think!

I read it again silently.

"Strange, isn't it?" Mom said.

"Sure is," Andie said, surveying the envelope again.

"Do you know anyone in Japan?" I asked.

"Certainly not," she said. "And it says I've known this person for a long time."

"That's not all," Andie said. "The person writing the letter must know Mr. Tate." She giggled, and so did I.

Mom seemed to know what we were getting at. "He can't help it he's bald."

"But what person in Japan knows you're dating Mr. Tate?" I asked.

Mom motioned us into the kitchen. "Could there be another Susan Meredith?"

"No chance," I said. "This person even knows about your divorce. See, here it says, 'Please remember to laugh like in the old days.' " I shivered. "Ooh, it's almost spooky."

Andie had an idea. "If you really do get another letter soon, Holly and I will be glad to read that one and discuss it with you, too." Mischief glinted in her dark eyes.

"Thanks, I'll keep that in mind," Mom said, playing along. "You'll be my correspondence consultants." She looked at the clock above the refrigerator. "How late do you girls plan to be up?"

"Not too late," I said, leading Andie out of the room. "We have a couple more phone calls to make."

"Well, try to be extra quiet after ten. I'm getting up rather early tomorrow."

I stopped at the bottom of the stairs. "How come?"

"Mike and I are having breakfast downtown. We have some important things to discuss."

I frowned, glancing at Andie.

She mouthed the words silently, "Who's Mike?"

"Mr. Tate," I whispered, trudging up to my room, banging the door shut.

"What's wrong?" she asked, heading for the phone to call Jared.

"This could be the end of life as I know it." Mom and Mr. Tate were spending too much time together. I wished I had a Plan of the Hour to keep *them* apart!

4

The next morning I tried to push Mr. Tate out of my mind by going over the scheme Andie and I had cooked up last night: the Plan of the Hour.

Everything was set to go. With Paula coming over here at three o'clock, Kayla would have to baby-sit Carrie and little Stephie, taking them with her to practice volleyball at Danny's. Jared had seemed more than willing to visit Paula . . . over here. The plan was worth celebrating with waffles for breakfast.

Andie talked me into letting her make waffles. She poured the batter with the finesse of an elephant. It oozed out the sides of the waffle iron, creating a cooked-on batter mess. Mega-waffles, that's what they were, equal to twice the size of Mom's. One and a half was all I could eat.

When the phone rang, I raced to get it, sticky fingers and all. The line was full of static, like it was a bad connection or . . . long distance.

"Hello?"

Silence.

"Hello?" I repeated.

"Is this Holly Meredith?" a male voice asked.

"Who's calling?"

"Did your mother receive a letter from Japan this week?" the voice persisted, ignoring my question.

"Yes, but she's busy now. May I take a message?" I asked. There was static on the line.

"Please tell her I miss her," he said, the static growing louder. The voice was muffled, yet familiar.

Then, click, he was gone.

I flew to the kitchen, licking the stickiness off my fingers. "Andie, guess what!"

She spun around. "Who was that?"

"Japan just called, I mean, *someone* from Japan called. I think it was Mom's secret admirer. Except there was something strange about his voice."

"What about it?"

"It sounded familiar."

"Really?" Andie asked excitedly. "Who?"

"I'm not sure," I said, clearing the table. "Probably just my imagination, but wait'll I tell Mom." Then I froze in my tracks. "Hold everything. Is this perfect timing or what!"

"What are you talking about?" Andie asked, still stuffing her mouth.

"This is exactly what I need to help get Mr. Tate out of my life."

Andie groaned. "Another plan? Is that what you're dreaming up?"

"Don't worry, I won't need your help for *this* one. It's perfect."

Andie looked relieved. She cut another bite of waffle.

"Now . . . first things first," I said. "Paula will be here at three. While she's here, you sneak over to Danny's.

Remember to get a complete report of *everything.*"

"Well, if I know your little sister, she'll have Danny wrapped around her finger. He'll be giving *her* volleyball pointers before the afternoon's over." Andie grinned.

"It's perfect." I could almost see little Carrie charming Danny. "She's something else, but then, so is our cousin Stephanie."

"How old is your oldest cousin?" Andie asked.

"Stan's fifteen. He's already got his driver's permit. When Uncle Jack gets settled and school starts, I'll introduce you to all of them."

It was obvious Andie liked the idea of meeting Stan, even though she and Billy Hill hung out a lot at youth group and school. Situations like that were constantly changing for Andie.

She carried her plate to the sink. "How are you going to entertain the well-heeled Miss Paula while you wait for Jared to show up today?"

"Play Scrabble."

"Think you can beat her?" Andie rinsed the syrup off her plate.

"No problem," I boasted.

"I hear she gets A's in composition. Maybe you've met your match." Andie tossed her hair with a giggle and headed for the bathroom.

"Fabulous," I muttered, wishing it were Kayla I was playing instead of Paula. Beating Paula's twin in a game of words would make my day. No, it would make my school year, which was starting in a little over three weeks from now. Making every day count between now and the day after Labor Day—the first day of school—was urgent. If Kayla flirted her way between Danny and me, well, I wasn't sure if I could handle it. Losing out to a girl who had my body shape wouldn't be quite as bad as losing to a *woman*, which I'm sure Kayla and her shapely sister were by now.

We spent the rest of the morning playing games and watching TV. At two-thirty, Andie left to catch the city bus to Danny's neighborhood across town. I set out the Scrabble board, Webster's Dictionary, and two glasses of root beer downstairs in the family room. Then I sang and danced around to Holy Voltage, my favorite Christian rap group, while I waited for Paula.

♥　　♥　　♥

When the doorbell rang, I hurried to open it, expecting to see Paula. Instead, our mail carrier stood there with a package for me to sign for, accompanied by a stack of letters.

The package, it turned out, was from Sears. I set it aside for Mom and flipped through the envelopes, finding a letter from Daddy, one from Grandma Meredith, and one from my pen pal, Lucas Wadsworth Leigh.

I traced the LWL stamped inside the fancy blue seal on the back of the envelope. Why was he writing again before I answered his letter? I tore open the envelope to find out.

Dear Holly:

You may be surprised to receive this letter so soon after my most recent one. I'm writing about an idea I have for manuscript swapping. By that I mean, are you interested in reading and critiquing each other's stories? If you like this idea, please send one of your stories or essays along with your next letter, and I'll do the same.

I found it interesting, Holly, that you have collected the entire mystery series for children by my aunt, Marty Leigh. Not many women are so sentimental as to save their childhood books. I like that. Perhaps I can arrange to have her autograph them for you the next time she's in Colorado.

I'll look forward to hearing from you. Happy writing!

Lucas W. Leigh

P.S. Could you send a list of your work (sort of a résumé), whether published or not?

I pulled on my hair, twisting it hard. Lucas actually thought I was a grown woman with a beloved collection of children's books. Not too surprising; after all, I'd led him to think I was much older than thirteen. I forced the guilt feelings away.

Checking my watch, I almost wished Paula wouldn't be arriving in a minute. I'd much rather work on my "résumé" for Lucas, proving what a mature person—*woman*—I really was. Then I remembered the reason why I'd invited Paula over in the first place, and held my breath. My clever plan *had* to work!

By the time the doorbell rang again, I was a wreck. Paula was late, and I worried Jared would show up at the same time, making her very suspicious.

Quickly, I headed for the door, ready to welcome Paula Miller inside. But the words stuck in my throat as I opened the door. There, on either side of Paula, stood my little sister, Carrie, and my cousin Stephanie!

I stared at them in disbelief.

"Ho-l-ly," Carrie sang, her hand on her hip, "aren't you going to let us in?"

"Uh, sorry," I said, stepping aside. Then, remembering my manners, I greeted Paula.

Carrie lugged her overnight gear inside, dumping it on the living room floor. Then she and Stephie disappeared upstairs.

Dumbfounded, I hustled Paula downstairs to the family room. I'd completely overlooked the chance of something like *this* happening. Why hadn't I realized Paula would bring the girls here with her, freeing Kayla up to meet with Danny? A best friend would do that. So would a twin sister.

"Want to play Scrabble?" I asked.

"I'd love to," she said, tucking her long hair behind her ears.

I began explaining the rules, going over every possible aspect of the game. "Any questions?" I asked.

"That was very good, Holly, but my sister and I play Scrabble all the time," she said, her voice sounding exactly like Kayla's.

I swallowed hard, embarrassed. Along with mismanaging the Plan of the Hour, I'd made a fool of myself, too.

But Paula let me off the hook by complimenting me on my hair. "It's so long and thick," she said. "I bet you can fix it a zillion different ways."

A *zillion*? That was *my* word.

I nodded, wondering what was happening at Danny's house right now. Was Kayla smiling at him too much? Making him forget *our* friendship?

Uneasy about what I didn't know, I started the game. Paula knew Scrabble, all right. After three turns she was ahead by ten points. I was so caught up in the game, an hour passed like five minutes. At last, I'd met my match.

Upstairs, I heard Mom getting her peppermint tea

ready. "Holly-Heart? You here?" she called.

"Downstairs," I said.

"It's raining so hard, the streets are flooded," she said. "That's why I'm late."

I'd hardly noticed the rain or that Mom was late getting home. This was the closest game I'd ever played. While I slid the tiles around on the rack, trying to make a word to outdo Paula, I suddenly remembered Andie.

Yikes! She was outdoors in this mess—sneaking around—spying at Danny's house. She was probably soaked to the skin by now. No good. Her ordeal in the Arkansas River last Tuesday had left her with a bad case of the sniffles.

"Excuse me a second, Paula," I said, leaving the Scrabble game. "I have to talk to my mom."

Mom was squeezing honey from the plastic bear when I raced into the kitchen. "It's an emergency," I began. "Andie's outside in the rain."

She looked at me funny. "Make sense, Holly. Why is Andie out in *this* weather?"

I pulled a stool away from the bar and plopped onto it. "This is terrible. Everything's wrong. *Everything!*"

"Why don't you start over, Holly-Heart . . . from the beginning."

I took a deep breath. It was no use. Besides, I could hear someone's footsteps on the front porch. I stood up to answer the door.

It was Jared Wilkins.

"Is Paula here?" he asked, his blue eyes eager to gaze on the brunette beauty, no doubt.

"In the family room. We were just playing Scrabble," I said, noticing his clothes were dry. "Did you get a ride?"

"Yeah, Danny's dad dropped me off."

"You were at Danny's?" I felt a tingle of hope.

"Just for a minute. Had to drop off a DVD I borrowed. That's when the rain started, so his dad offered me a ride over here. Weird, though, we saw Andie walking in the rain. She was drenched, so we picked her up and took her home."

I felt lousy about Andie, but glad the rain cut Kayla's practice session with Danny short.

Jared asked, "What was Andie doing across town in the rain?"

I ignored his question. No need for him to know how badly my plan had flopped. "How's Danny doing?"

Jared grinned. "I'll give it to you straight. Kayla seemed pleased about the sudden change in weather when we left."

"What does *that* mean?" I tugged hard on my hair.

"Well, think how *you'd* feel," he taunted.

I shifted my gaze, staring at the overnight bag Carrie had left on the floor. It was none of Jared's business how I felt about Danny Myers.

"Why don't you go down and finish the Scrabble game with Paula?" I suggested, trying to hide my despair.

Jared ran his fingers through his hair as he headed downstairs. I followed close behind, noticing how surprised Paula looked when she saw him.

"Do you mind if I leave you two alone for a sec?" I said, realizing how silly that probably sounded.

Jared jumped right on it. "Take your time."

I raced upstairs to the phone.

"Andie?" I said when she answered. "Are you okay?"

"Sort of." She sounded all stuffed up. "You won't like what I have to tell you."

"I already know," I said. "Jared's here."

She sneezed. "There's more. Kayla and Danny had a snack together at Danny's house. His mom served it to them in the breakfast nook."

"How do you know?"

"I stood under the trees in the neighbor's yard and watched through the windows." Andie coughed and blew her nose.

"Then what?"

"Danny's mom went out on the porch, tending her flowers, leaving Kayla alone with Danny for a while."

"Oh great." I could almost picture Kayla batting her made-up eyes at Danny.

"I'm sorry, Holly. Looks like our plan fell through."

"No kidding," I whispered. "What a nightmare!"

5

I turned a page in my diary and wrote: *Saturday, August 14. The Plan of the Hour failed . . . absolutely and totally failed, right down to the second it rained, forcing Danny and Kayla indoors. Some cozy setup for Miss Kayla Miller.*

It was nearly time for supper. Paula and Jared had just left, and I was pouring out my pent-up feelings of the day on lined paper. I felt sorry for girls who didn't write in journals. It was the best way to handle life sometimes. And what about people who didn't talk to God? How did *they* cope?

Sliding off my window seat, I sat cross-legged on the floor. Bearie-O fell forward, his droopy eyes looking sadder than ever. I smiled at him. "Hi-ya, Bearie-O. Are you feeling sad because I do?"

I moved his head to make him nod.

"You're the best bear a girl could own."

"You don't *own* him," Carrie said, startling me.

"What are you doing in my room?" I snapped.

She covered her mouth with her hands, but the giggles poured out. Then Stephanie stepped out from behind her.

"You! *Both* of you are in trouble," I shouted. "Why do you keep breaking the rules? You don't see me in *your* room, do you, Carrie?"

Stephanie disappeared quickly, leaving Carrie only half grinning in the fading light of evening.

"We heard you talking in the dark. It was Stephie's idea to sneak in. Honest, Holly."

"You're *older* than Stephie. Better spell out the rules of our house to her," I said, putting Bearie-O back on his shelf.

"It's dark in here." She flicked on the light switch. "Why are you sitting in the dark talking to your stuffed animals?"

"None of your business."

"Fine, don't tell me," she said. "But I've got a message for you from Mommy. She wants you to set the table. Mr. Tate and Zachary are coming for supper." Carrie left, closing the door behind her.

I stomped over to the light switch. Sitting in the dark was good for the soul sometimes. Maybe when Carrie grew up she'd understand.

Opening the bottom drawer of my dresser, I slid my journal into its hiding place. My notebook of secret prayers was underneath. So were copies of my letters to pen pals, including Lucas Wadsworth Leigh, all stored in an old legal file, a reject from the law firm where Mom was a paralegal. Another folder held *his* letters to me. Writing an answer to his last letter would be my first project tonight after supper.

This whole thing of "snail mail" pen pals had been Andie's idea. She was so bored last month, she challenged me to a contest. "Let's see who can get the most pen pals before school starts," she'd said. "And no fair getting extra money from parents for postage."

Andie was like that. Very bossy.

Not wanting to miss out on the fun, I had agreed. Soon I was ahead with six pen friends. Then she moved ahead, adding two girls from Panama. Quickly, I sent off for a girl in Salzburg. Tied!

Counting Lucas, I was actually winning. But for some reason, keeping this *male* pal a secret from Andie was important to me.

One week after Andie's challenge, I had discovered Lucas Leigh's name in the personal ads in a writer's magazine at the library.

Lucas Wadsworth Leigh, nephew to mystery writer Marty Leigh, is interested in corresponding with aspiring female fiction writers, the ad read.

I couldn't resist. Marty Leigh was tops. I owned every book she'd ever written. If she was even remotely related to this Lucas person, well . . . I had to know more. So I sent my first letter off to Lucas W. Leigh.

Promptly, I received a letter back. A fancy seal was affixed to the back of the envelope with LWL on display in calligraphy, as if he were royalty or something.

Luckily, I hadn't declared my age to be thirteen. That might've spoiled everything, because LWL, as I soon discovered, was a *junior in college!*

I hadn't lied when I answered his letter, just kept the truth concealed. What difference did age make, anyway? Andie's daring nature was beginning to rub off on me.

"Holly!" called Carrie. "Mom's waiting."

I pushed my dresser drawer shut, wishing I could put it under lock and key. Especially with an immature younger sister and giggly cousin snooping around. "Coming, Mom,"

I called as I hurried downstairs.

Delicious aromas filled the kitchen. Mom had baked meat loaf with her yummy brown sugar and ketchup topping. And there were two yellow candles lying on the counter.

"What's the occasion?" I asked suspiciously.

Mom motioned for me to help. "Time to dish up."

"Celebrating Zachary's remission?" I asked.

"Good idea," she said, evading my question.

"Mom, you're not announcing something important, are you?" I held the forks in my right hand, suspended in time and space, waiting . . .

Please, dear God, don't let this be what I'm thinking.

I turned to face her, my heart beating wildly. Did I dare tell her what I thought of Mr. Tate becoming her husband?

The doorbell rang. "It's Mike and Zachary." Mom rushed to the door the way I might have if Danny were awaiting me on the porch.

My heart sank. Was Mom in love?

I wanted to scatter the utensils around the dining room table. Instead I forced myself to fold the napkins neatly, placing *two* forks to the left of each plate.

"Hi, girls," Zach said, lugging a duffel bag full of toy planes and missiles and things. It was good to see him looking so cheerful. And healthy.

"Hungry?" I asked him.

He sniffed the air. "Smells good." He plopped down at the head of the table.

Mr. Tate carried a square white box. Zach pointed to it, acting excited about what was inside.

"What's in there?" Carrie asked, touching the lid.

"Uh, *that's* a surprise," Mr. Tate said, shooing her away.

I hoped it wasn't a wedding cake. The excitement in my mother's eyes worried me. She'd met Mr. Tate for breakfast early this morning. Had she gone and eloped?

With a grand wave of her hand, Mom announced, "Please be seated, everyone. Look for your name card beside each plate."

Name cards? This *was* special.

Zach found his place, next to Mom. Stephie was on the other side of her. Mr. Tate sat at the head of the table, the empty spot where Daddy used to sit years ago.

Mom carried the food to the table. Then Mr. Tate prayed without Mom asking, like he was in charge or something.

When the baked potatoes came around, I unwrapped the foil from mine, scrunching it into a ball. "Please pass the butter," I said.

I watched, almost jealously, as Mom worked first on Zach's potato, then Stephie's. She seemed so fond of Zach.

Mr. Tate waited for everyone to start eating before he tapped his fork lightly on his water glass. "I'd like to propose a toast."

Propose? Sounded scary.

He held up his glass. "Children, this is a toast to our new life together as a family. Susan, this is a toast to our new investment endeavor."

Mom looked scared, like something had just dawned on her. "Ah, wait a minute, Mike," she said. "I thought you were going to give me time to discuss this with the girls."

Mr. Tate lowered his glass. "You'd like their permission?" He looked at Carrie, then me. "Well, girls. What do you think?"

Carrie grinned. "When are you getting married?"

Mr. Tate's eyes shone. "Soon," he said, gazing at Mom.

Carrie smiled. "Goody. I'll have a brother," she said, pointing to Zach, who grabbed his throat, pretending to gag.

"Calm down, young man," Mr. Tate reprimanded him. "Your little friend is only being polite."

Now *I* felt like I might choke. Mr. Tate was much too serious. Couldn't he take a joke?

Mr. Tate turned and smiled at me. "How do you feel about this news, Holly, uh, Heart, is it?"

I coughed, despising him for putting me on the spot like this. Where were *his* manners?

"Excuse me, please," I said, leaving the table and rushing to the bathroom.

"Holly?" Mom called. "Are you all right, dear?"

All right was for kids with boring, uneventful lives. Kids with a dad who lived with them. Kids who didn't have to worry about possible stepfathers like Mr. Tate. Not kids like me.

I closed the door to the bathroom. Locked inside, I felt like I was drowning. Now I knew how Andie had felt with the mighty Arkansas River rushing around her. Pulling her into its powerful current. Grabbing her, thrusting her into its whirling waves, while she worked . . . pounding, thrashing . . . fighting to survive.

Exhausted, I sat on the edge of the tub. Why was *I* fighting so hard? This was *Mom's* choice. If Mr. Tate was right for her, why did I dislike him?

A light tapping came at the door. "Holly-Heart, it's me, Mom."

"I'm okay," I said, knowing full well that I preferred to stay in here, nursing my pain for the rest of my life.

"You don't sound okay," she said.

Mom was persistent—one of the many things I loved about her. She always knew when I needed to be alone, and when I needed her there, even the times I told her to leave me alone

"Honey?" She was still waiting.

The tears came, so I couldn't answer. Besides, I didn't want to spoil her special night.

"Something must be very wrong," she said. "Are you sick?"

Oh yeah, I was sick, all right. Sick for all the years I'd missed Daddy. Sick that he left in the first place. Sick that he'd remarried. Sick that if Mr. Tate and Mom got together, Daddy would never be able to marry Mom again if he ever had the chance.

I ran the hot and cold water together. Fast. I blew my nose and muttered something about joining her for dessert.

"Are you sure, Holly?" She knew me well.

"Yes," I managed to say, turning the water off.

I heard her footsteps fade away as she went back downstairs. I wiped my face. A touch of blush came off on the washcloth. I stared at it. There were no M's for Meredith on these towels like the M's for Myers at Danny's house. The stuck-up Miller twins probably had monogrammed M's on *their* towels, too.

What if someone gave Mom a wedding gift of towels with T for Tate stitched on them? Instantly, I knew I would never, ever use those towels if we got any. My last name was *Meredith*, and nothing could change that.

Slowly, I took a deep breath and opened the bathroom door. One by one, I descended the stairs.

Everyone was almost finished eating. I sat down and

picked at my meat loaf, feeling Carrie's eyes on me. My mascara was probably smudged. At least I was allowed to wear it, even if it *was* the lightest brown ever made.

Wearing makeup was part of the growing-up ritual and a privilege, Mom had said. *This* minute, however, I wished I was a little girl again, with Daddy sitting across from me at the head of the table.

Mom made small talk until I finally finished eating. Then Mr. Tate brought the white box over, setting it down in the middle of the table. I held my breath, certain there'd be a layer cake with white posted curlicues dancing around the edges. And a miniature bride and groom smiling on the tip-top.

Slowly, he reached inside the box and lifted the plate up. "This," he said, "is a honeycomb."

I stared at the tiny cubicles of wax.

Mr. Tate cut a small portion off and gave it to Mom. One after another we were served the waxy stuff, heavy with honey.

Next came a demonstration. Mr. Tate picked up a bite-sized piece and began to chew it. "You work the honey out of the comb and spit out the wax."

"That's gross," said Carrie.

Zach was getting the hang of it, however. "Mmm, it's good."

Mom beamed down at Zach, putting her arm around him. "It's good for you," she said. Then, looking around the table, "It's good for *all* of us."

"Which brings me to some exciting news." Mr. Tate sat down and directed his gaze to me. "Your mother and I are planning to purchase some land north of here."

Mom nodded. "We spoke to a real-estate broker during breakfast this morning."

North of here? I swallowed hard. The *mountains* were north of here.

Mr. Tate continued, "This five-acre plot of land we're considering is a choice spot for a log home. And the perfect place for a bee farm, among other things."

Carrie's eyes widened. "Bees make honey. We're going to have bees?"

"Yes, we're going to become beekeepers and gather honey. And," he paused, breathing deeply, "get in touch with nature."

I stared at this man. Not only did he want to marry my mother, he wanted to ruin my life!

6

I managed to speak at last, addressing only Mom. "Why do we have to move?"

"We don't *have* to, Holly," she said firmly. "But things are better in the country, uh, in the mountains. The air is cleaner and—"

Mr. Tate interrupted. "There are certain things you don't know, Holly. Your mother and I will discuss them with you in private." Here, he glanced at Zachary, who was picking the waxy honeycomb out of his teeth.

Anger boiled in me. Then Mom suggested Carrie and I clear the table. Gladly. Anything to get away from this man. Mr. Tate was turning out to be someone great to hate.

"We'll have family devotions in one hour," he announced.

I looked at Carrie. "Family devotions?" I whispered.

"Yeah, isn't it cool? Zach's gonna be our brother."

Stunned at her response, I opened the dishwasher. Carrie, my own flesh and blood, was in favor of this nightmare.

I waited till Mr. Tate left the room. A sad lump stuck in my throat as Zach put his arm around *my* mother. Together, they headed downstairs to the family room.

I grabbed Carrie's arm. "Listen to me. This is serious."

"Ouch, you're hurting me," she wailed.

"I am not," I said, letting go.

"Holly, what's wrong with you?"

"I'm worried. Mom's going to marry Mr. Tate and move us out of the city. We'll leave this house—Daddy's house— and live in some drafty log cabin where we won't even have our own bedrooms and we'll have to gather honey and berries for food like the pilgrims."

Carrie stared at me. "I'm telling. You're wrong . . . that's not what we're gonna do." And she raced downstairs, whining the whole time.

Betrayed. That's how I felt. I couldn't even share my greatest fears with my sister. She was off blabbing it to Mom and Mr. Tate this minute.

So what. Let her tell. And when I got in trouble for expressing my opinion, I'd announce that I was staying in Dressel Hills. Maybe Danny's rich parents would adopt me. Or there was always Andie. I rinsed and stacked the dishes, drawing the water for the pots and pans.

Just then Carrie came stomping up the steps. "They want to talk to you after the kitchen's clean, but before devotions." She seemed to enjoy ordering me around.

"You have an attitude problem, Carrie," I retorted. "Go play with Stephie."

"I can't. She's going back to the Millers' house to-night."

"Well, then, go do something else, unless you want to scrub these pans." I knew *that* would make her disappear. And I was right. She skipped out of the room.

Watching the minute hand on the clock above the

fridge, I became more and more furious. Mom was supposed to be on *my* side. But it was obvious she was attached to Zachary. Sure, he was a motherless cancer patient, but now that he was in remission couldn't she pay attention to her *own* kids for a change?

I tried to force the Tate-hate away by concentrating on the good things in my life, like Andie and her surviving the icy Arkansas River, and how loyal she'd been, standing out in the rain for me. And school starting soon, and volleyball tryouts just around the corner.

And there was my secret pen pal, Lucas Wadsworth Leigh. What a cool name. It even sounded like an author, a literary one at that. I could hardly wait to write back to him. I had planned to tonight after supper, but that was before Mr. Tate ordered family devotions.

"Holly," Mom said, now in the kitchen.

Startled, I jumped. "Hew long have you been standing there?"

"Not long."

I rinsed off the meat loaf pan, wondering how long I'd scrubbed the same spot. "You wanted to talk to me?"

"*We* do," she said. "When you're finished."

"Mom?" I hesitated. "I don't want to live in the mountains. Can't we stay here?" I dried my hands.

"Mike and I have already made an offer on the property. It's truly beautiful up there, you'll see."

"I don't want to see. It's too far away. Besides, how will I get to school?"

"Those are things we'll discuss. Perhaps we can get a permit for you to continue at your school. It won't happen immediately. We'll have to build the house first, and winter's coming on soon."

Three cheers for winter. For *anything* that would slow down this ridiculous process.

"Let's talk downstairs," she said, putting her arm around me.

Mr. Tate was fooling with the sound system installed in our entertainment center. He pushed the Play button on the CD player. Holy Voltage interrupted the stillness. He jerked his bald head back, glaring at me. "What in the world is *that?*"

It was time to defend myself. "That's Christian rap. It's totally cool."

Mr. Tate frowned. "Cool? Let's have something soothing instead." He fumbled around with the system, obviously confused.

I waited, prolonging his frustration. The heavy rap beat made me want to dance across the room and turn up the volume so he could *really* get the message. It *was* a Christian group, after all.

A pleading look crossed his face. "Please turn it off, Holly."

In a flash, I pressed the correct button, wondering if this was how things would be when Mr. Tate was forever calling the shots.

He sat on the chair across from me. "There are some things you need to know about Zachary's remission, Holly," he began. "It is difficult for the doctors to project into the future. Of course, we're hoping for the best. But the best might only be a few years."

What does this have to do with anything? I wondered.

Mom continued, "We want to change our way of living, for Zach's sake. Perhaps prolong his life with the way we eat and things like that."

"The stress in the city alone can add to a person's susceptibility to disease," Mr. Tate stated.

Oh please, I thought. Dressel Hills was barely a city. A ski village of ten thousand people wasn't stressful in the least.

"We'll have our own raw honey as well as plant herbs for teas," Mom said.

This didn't sound like the mother I knew and loved. The only herbs she cared about were in the tea bags she used to make peppermint tea every day after work. And honey . . . what was wrong with the stuff in our plastic bear?

"You're so quiet, Holly," Mom said.

I was thinking hard. "What about your long drive to work?" I asked.

"That's something else that must be considered," she said.

"Are you quitting?" I asked.

Mr. Tate responded with amazing speed. "Your mother has worked to support this family for a number of years. It's time for her to stay home and care for the family. Zach will continue to need attention as time goes on."

Funny, he mentioned only Zach.

"When will all this happen?" I asked, scared silly.

"It's likely that your mother and I will marry before the house is built. Perhaps before the holidays."

"Which holidays?" There were a string of them coming up.

"Maybe Christmas," Mom offered. "It will give us plenty of time to plan."

Mr. Tate leaned forward. The light bounced off his shiny head. At that moment I remembered the joke in

Mom's mystery letter from Japan. Mr. Tate really *didn't* have any locks.

Here we sat in the family room, on the verge of altering our lives forever, while someone halfway around the world was reminding Mom to laugh like in the old days. And the phone call! How could I have forgotten to tell her?

Faster than lightning, I remembered my plan. Better than the Plan of the Hour, *this* one—the Plan to Save the Meredith Family—might just spare us from becoming Tate bait.

I summoned my courage with a deep breath. "Mom, I forgot to tell you about a long-distance phone call that came today."

She studied me. "Who called?"

"The man from Japan who sent you the letter."

Her eyes squinted. She glanced at Mr. Tate, who was suddenly all ears. A strange expression crossed her face. It seemed to relay a secret message for me only. Mom wanted me to drop the subject. Immediately. For some reason, she did not want Mike Tate to know about the letter.

Perfect! How could I resist a chance like this? By ignoring Mom's facial plea, maybe, just maybe, I'd set things in motion to win my family back. It was a risk worth taking.

I continued, "The caller asked if you'd received his letter."

"What's she talking about?" Mr. Tate asked. It was amazing how fast he played into my hands.

"Mom has a secret admirer," I announced. "He lives in Japan, but he speaks perfect English."

Mr. Tate chuckled a little. "A secret admirer, eh, Susan?" He got up and sauntered across the room to Mom, squatting down beside her chair. "What about this mystery man in your life?"

This was the first time in months I'd seen them this close. Usually it was *Zach* Mom was hugging.

I sneaked out of the room, confident I'd started something Mom couldn't finish . . . not without pulling Mr. Tate right into the middle of things.

Right where I wanted him.

7

Dear Lucas, I began writing my letter in the privacy of my bedroom. *I am very much interested in exchanging stories.* I hoped this sounded grown-up enough to convince him to continue writing. Surprisingly, he hadn't pushed for personal info, such as my age. But he assumed I was much older. Maybe it was my writing style. After all, I could write as well as any college student around.

I've enclosed a short story for you to critique, and I hope you'll do the same in your next letter. There. Now he would know I was sincerely interested in writing.

For fun, I chose "Love Times Two" as a sample of some of my best fiction. It had been an English assignment last school year. The main character in the story was really me, and the sister was really Andie. In the story—and in real life—we were madly in love with the same guy. After she heard me read it, Andie had accused me of describing her "down to her toenails"—among other things. Still, it was a fabulous story.

The A+ and the heading—*7th-grade English*—had to go, of course. A college man wouldn't be caught dead writing to a thirteen-year-old.

Rewriting the story on Mom's computer, I found several things to revise. By the time it was done, I was prouder than ever.

Then I continued the letter. *Please tell me more about your aunt, Marty Leigh. I have admired her work for years and began collecting her books when I was only a child.* It was true. Under twelve, you're a kid. I had read that somewhere. Besides, I'd received my first Marty Leigh mystery book on my eleventh birthday.

As for arranging to have her autograph my collection, well, it's not necessary. But thanks for the kind offer. That got me off the hook in case Lucas told Marty Leigh about the "woman" in Dressel Hills who owned all her books. What a surprise it would be for her to discover me, a skinny little eighth-grader.

You'll find my list of works at the bottom of this page. The list would take a while to put together, so I set the letter aside.

Everything I'd written in my entire life was in the bottom dresser drawer, in a lavender file folder. There were essays and fantasies; secret prayer lists and secret journals; letters to pen pals, and letters to imaginary people—famous and otherwise. There were also plans for surviving junior high, such as:

Plan A
Plan B (next best)
Plan C (if all else fails)

Next came the Loyalty Papers—guidelines for conducting a best friendship. Andie and I had written them in grade school. Only the copy remained. The original documents had been ripped to shreds after a fight Andie and I had last spring.

Poetry by the pages spilled out. And short stories—mysteries, romance, drama. Lucas had requested a list of my work, published or not. That included more than just fiction. So I set out to alphabetize my "work."

Halfway through, the phone rang. Mom called up the steps. "Holly, it's for you. Danny Myers is on the line."

Danny? Yes! I dashed to the phone in Mom's room. "Hey, Danny," I said.

"What are you doing?" he asked.

"Sorting through some of my old papers."

"Like what?"

"Oh, just some stories and poems and things I wrote."

"Sounds like fun. Maybe I could read them sometime." It sounded like he was asking.

"Sure, I'd like that," I said, wondering why he'd called.

"When do you want to practice for volleyball tryouts?"

I caught my breath. He still wanted to help me after spending a cozy rainy afternoon with stuck-up Kayla. "When's a good time for you?" I said, trying not to sound too anxious. Or surprised.

"I'm free next Saturday. Will that work for you?"

"Okay. Where?"

"Let's meet at school. The gymnasium will be open. It'll be good for you to practice where the tryouts are held," he suggested.

"Good idea," I said.

"See you Saturday around two o'clock."

I said thanks and good-bye and hung up. Immediately, I called Andie.

"Hello?" Mrs. Martinez answered.

"May I please speak to Andie?"

"She's not feeling well, Holly. Is there something you want me to tell her?"

"I hope she feels better soon," I said. "Tell her that."

"She'll be sorry she missed your call. Good-bye."

Poor Andie. Standing out in the rain this afternoon hadn't helped. And it was my fault.

The doorbell rang. It was probably Kayla and Paula's mom coming to pick up Stephanie. I went back to my résumé, Bearie-O keeping me company on the floor.

I figured the minute Mr. Tate and Zachary left to go home, Mom would approach me about my big mouth. Why should a silly letter from Japan cause a problem between Mom and me?

Japan. Hmm, might be an interesting place for me to have a pen pal. One who could read and write English, though. As far as I knew, Andie hadn't added any more pen pals. But there were only twenty-three days left before school started on September seventh.

"Who wants ice cream?" Carrie yelled from the kitchen at the top of her lungs.

"I do!" I left my project on the floor and zipped down the steps.

Carrie helped Mom dish up some chocolate ice cream. We sat at the bar as Mom looked at me, her eyes squinted half shut. Her eyes spelled trouble.

I blurted out, "I shouldn't have told Mr. Tate about the letter, I guess." I hoped to get this conversation over so I could finish my letter to Lucas.

"You guess?" Mom's eyes narrowed even more.

"I could tell you didn't want me to say anything about it. But why, Mom? What's the big deal?"

"*This* is the big deal. Mike has a tremendous amount of stress right now. With Zachary and other things."

"So he's too busy to have fun, is that what you're saying?"

Mom looked tired, confused. "Right now, Mike doesn't need to think there's someone else in my life."

"But there *is*," I said. "And it's not a mystery letter writer from Japan. It's Zachary. He's right in the middle of everything—the person you're always with when Mr. Tate's over here. I think he's a cute kid, too, but I wouldn't marry his dad just to give him a mother."

Mom stared at me for a moment, leaning on her elbows.

Carrie got up and stroked Mom's back. "Holly doesn't really mean it, Mommy. She's all mixed up."

We sat there without saying a word. At last I felt so uneasy I said, "The ice cream is melting."

Mom spooned up some of hers, glaring at me. "Lately, Holly, ever since your trip to see your father, I feel you've been trying to interfere in my life. I gave you a chance to exercise your independence this summer. Is this what I get in return?"

"That's not fair," I shot back. "And it's not just *your* life with Mr. Tate. It's ours, too."

"And Zach's," Carrie added, scampering out of the room.

"Now's not the time to discuss this," Mom said. "I have a very early day tomorrow."

"What, another romantic breakfast?" I scoffed.

"Holly, that's quite enough." She got up to rinse the empty ice-cream bowls.

I gritted my teeth. "I am not going to let you marry Mr. Tate just because you feel sorry for his kid."

She whirled around. "We have plans to buy property together. We signed a *contract*."

"Get your name off it. You're a paralegal; you know how to reverse legal documents."

"Holly, listen! I'm not interested in getting out of anything. Do you hear me? I am going to marry Mike Tate." Her face looked almost stern as her blue eyes squinted shut.

Tears spilled down my cheeks as I turned to run upstairs. Carrie was sneaking away from my room as I reached the top step. My important papers still lay on the floor. All but my journal. Carrie had broken our rule again. I wanted to scream at her as I searched for it.

I heard the bathtub water running. Jumping up, I dashed to the bathroom door. "You'll be sorry, Carrie Meredith," I shouted, pounding on the door. "Tell me where you put it. Now!" I kept pounding my fist on the door. "Did you hear me?"

Mom came upstairs. "Holly, what's going on?"

"Carrie's been in my room again. She stole my diary," I sobbed.

"I'll handle this," Mom said, leaning against the door. "Carrie, do you know anything about Holly's diary?"

"I didn't take it," came the tiny voice.

I shouted back, between tears, "Yes, you did. Or else you would've answered me before."

"I was scared of you before," Carrie said, opening the bathroom door a crack.

Mom turned, casting a disapproving look my way. "Holly, let it go for now. Okay?"

"But it's the most important thing I own," I cried. "I can't live without my journal."

I ran to my room, flinging myself across the bed. It seemed like the end of the world.

8

I don't know how long I buried my face in the pillow. A good cry sometimes helps make things seem less disastrous. Still, I vowed I'd get my diary back, no matter what.

Anger for Mr. Tate simmered in me, too. I was determined to do whatever it took to save my family from him. It might be easier than I thought, especially since I was sure Mom wasn't in love with him. Downstairs, I had waited to hear her use love as a reason for marriage.

But she never had.

Wiping my tear-stained face, I knew she'd thank me someday for interfering.

Just then Mom peeked her head through the doorway. "Carrie has something to tell you, Holly-Heart."

Carrie crept around the door, shyly. "I'm sorry I snooped in your room, Holly, but I never touched your diary, honest." She disappeared before I could say a word.

I leaped off my bed and ran after her, into the hall. "Carrie, I'm sorry, too. I didn't mean to scare you. You know I'd never hurt you."

Her eyes grew big. "But you kept pounding on the door.

I thought you were going to break it down."

"I was angry at you because you broke our rule."

"I won't do it again. I promise," she said.

Mom held the hair dryer, motioning to Carrie to finish drying her long hair.

"Good night, Carrie," I called after her. "I love you."

Back in my bedroom, I searched for my diary under an ocean of stories and paper on the floor. My back ached as I sorted through all the spiral notebooks in my drawer. And then there it was, in its usual place.

I hurried to tell Mom and Carrie. "It was right where I always keep it," I said.

Carrie got a mischievous look in her eyes. "Where . . . where? Just kidding," she said, laughing.

"Remember, you promised," I said, pointing my finger at her.

"I know," Carrie said as Mom braided her hair.

I put my hand in the small of my back as I headed to my room. The pain nagged at me. Maybe it came from leaning over so long, doing my résumé for Lucas Leigh.

I was too tired to finish alphabetizing my list of writings. There were more important things to do just now.

Reaching for my notebook full of secret prayer lists, I began writing a new page. Before I fell asleep tonight I would ask God to keep Mom from marrying Mr. Tate.

♥   ♥   ♥

The next morning I dragged out of bed before anyone else. Even though I'd slept ten hours, I still felt groggy.

Smoothing the sheets, I noticed a spot.

Yes! My body clock hadn't stopped ticking after all. I'd become a young woman during the night.

High in my closet, there were personal supplies waiting for this moment. On my way to get them, I posed in front of the mirror. Andie was right, I *did* have more going for me than just my long hair. I was developing, too.

Wait, what was that on my chin? I leaned close to the mirror. A pimple had emerged overnight, too. Andie had warned me about such nasties.

I couldn't wait to tell her my big news.

Carrie was sound asleep when I peeked in her room, so I tiptoed to the kitchen. Some toast and a bowl of cereal was all I needed while I finished my résumé and letter to Lucas Leigh.

P.S. I think I know what you mean about cars and smooth riding, I wrote. *A friend of mine owns a new SUV, and it's very cool.*

I didn't know exactly how I would respond if Lucas inquired about the car I drove. Maybe by that time, he'd be so impressed with my manuscripts, my age wouldn't matter. I could only hope so. Keeping part of the truth back was strange to me, yet exciting. Still, it made me jittery.

I licked a stamp anyway, positioning it squarely in the corner of my envelope. Then I hid it upstairs in my bottom drawer.

I sat on my window seat by the open window, breathing in the early morning air. Mr. Tate's talk about fresh mountain air was pathetic. Fresh air was all around us, right here. There was no escaping it. And moving to a higher elevation wouldn't help Zachary. In the mountains it was harder to breathe; there was *less* oxygen. Zach was just a feeble excuse to move us away from Dressel Hills.

I showered and dressed for church, singing songs from last spring's choir tour, hoping to chase thoughts of Mr. Tate out of my mind. It was a day to celebrate my graduation from girlhood.

Using the hall phone, I dialed Andie. "Are you too sick to go to church?" I asked.

"I'm staying home," she said, coughing. "But you can come over this afternoon. Just don't catch what I have and miss out on your volleyball practice with Danny."

"How'd you know about *that*?" I asked.

"Paula Miller told me. She said Danny called her sister last night and mentioned it."

"He called Kayla? I wonder what about?" I asked.

"Probably something about volleyball tryouts. Who knows? Just don't freak. Danny likes *you* best, I guarantee it."

"Right," I mumbled into the phone.

"Remember, Billy and Danny are good friends, and Billy and I talk," Andie said.

"And exactly what are you holding out on me?" I asked.

She laughed in spite of her clogged nasal passages. "Wait and see."

"Speaking of waiting, *I* have major news," I said.

"Betcha not as big as my news."

"Bigger," I said. "But I can't tell you now."

"When?"

"Later."

"Aw, tell me real quick," she begged.

"Guess we're even." I giggled. "See you." I hung up the phone.

With a sudden burst of energy, I dashed to Carrie's

room. She was in bed, still asleep, looking like the angel in the Christmas storybook Daddy had given us years ago. One arm was draped over the mermaid Mr. Tate had given her.

I wondered about our future—Carrie's and mine. Would Mom marry Mike Tate and become Zach's step-mother? Would I grow up to become Mrs. Danny Myers? Would there be a houseful of children? Maybe I'd be an author and keep my maiden name . . . or hyphenate it. Holly Meredith-Myers. Perfect. It even sounded famous. Our kids would travel with us as we went from one book signing to another. We'd hire a governess or a tutor or a . . .

Carrie woke up just then, sitting up in bed. "Why are you staring at me?" she asked in her sleepy, little-girl voice.

"Oh, was I? Just daydreaming, I guess."

She rubbed her eyes. "What time is it?"

"Time to get dressed for Sunday school."

"Where's Mom?"

"At church . . . teacher's meeting."

"Can we have French toast?" she asked.

"I already ate, but I'll make you some."

"With Mr. Tate's honey?" She grinned.

I wondered why he was the first thing on her mind this morning. "Is there any honey left?" I asked.

"There better be," she said, jumping out of bed.

"Meet you downstairs in ten minutes," I said, heading for the stairs.

♥   ♥   ♥

After a noon meal of pot roast and the works, I excused

myself since it was Carrie's turn to do the dishes. Fifteen minutes later, I was standing at Andie's front door. Her curly-haired brothers toddled near Andie's mom as she welcomed me inside.

"Hi, Chris and Jon," I said, leaning over to hug the twins.

"Andie's upstairs," Mrs. Martinez said, adjusting Jon's little blue suspenders. I took the steps two at a time.

"In here, Holly," Andie called to me from her room.

With the grace of a ballerina, I stepped into her bedroom. It was decorated in shades of pink. Streams of sunlight enhanced the colors as it poured into the window like a spotlight. Pausing there for a moment, I pulled my hair back dramatically, holding it up.

"*Now* what are you up to?" Andie said, laughing.

"Look closely. See anything different?" I posed this way and that, like a model.

Andie leaned on her arm, playing along. "Hmm, there's something new on your chin. Is that your first zit?"

I swung my hair around. "That doesn't count."

"Let your hair down and turn around," she said.

I did.

"Aagh!" she said, pretending to be shocked. "You've trimmed your hair."

I shook my head.

"Something *is* different," she said, scratching her head.

I stood up straighter. "Are you ready for this?" I said, prolonging the announcement.

"Out with it," she said.

"Feast your eyes on a full-fledged woman."

She let out a little squeal, jumped off her bed, and flung

her arms around me. She nearly knocked over the floor lamp beside her bean bag.

Andie's mom walked past her room just then, carrying one of the twins. "Everything okay in there?" she called.

"The monthly miracle! It's finally happened to you," Andie said, her brown eyes sparkling.

"Shh! Don't tell the whole world," I said, enjoying Andie's definition—the monthly miracle. It had a unique twist to it. Better than the birds and the bees.

Yikes . . . bees! They reminded me of Mr. Tate.

"Now, what's this news Billy told you about Danny and me?" I asked, changing the subject and going to sit on the bean bag.

Andie threw herself on the bed and lay there with a silly grin on her round face. "Danny likes you, and I mean a lot."

"Are you sure?"

"Billy said so." Andie propped herself up on one arm.

"Really?" I said, my heart in my throat. "What'll Kayla think when she finds out?"

"Just be ready for anything," Andie said, rolling over.

"I don't get it. I wouldn't try to break up a friendship *she* had with a church boy." I leaned forward.

Andie held up her hands. "Better stay away from me if you want to enjoy the last three weeks of summer vacation."

I pulled my T-shirt up over my nose. "How's that?"

Andie reached for a tissue, stuffing it up her left nostril. It hung down out of her nose while she sat there staring at me.

Finally I couldn't stand it any longer. "You're too much," I said, laughing hysterically.

"What a lousy way to spend the end of summer," she said, her voice more nasal sounding than before. "Hey, which reminds me, I just sent off for two more pen pals. And that makes *me* the winner of our contest."

"Not yet. There's still time," I insisted.

"Hey, we never planned the award for the winner. What should it be?" she asked.

"How about a year's worth of postage?"

"You must be running out of allowance money," she said, leaning against her hot-pink pillows.

"I can always baby-sit for Zach while Mr. Tate and Mom go house hunting."

"Sounds serious."

"Not for long." I was sure my Plan to Save the Meredith Family was the answer. Thank goodness for secret admirers and anonymous phone calls!

Five days passed. It was Friday, August twentieth, the day before my practice session with Danny Myers.

I stared at my clothes closet. Time for new stuff. Mom and I had planned to go clothes shopping next week for school, but I needed something new . . . soon.

A knock came at my door. "Enter," I said, holding up two pairs of jeans.

Carrie held a stack of mail. "Looks like you got something from Lucas," she said.

"Who?"

"LWL." She grinned.

"Sit down," I said sternly, pointing her to sit on my window seat. "How do you know about him?"

"Uh, that night I sneaked in here, I read your letter from him."

I squinted my eyes, like Mom. "You better keep this quiet, you hear?"

"What's the big secret?" she asked.

"It's not a secret," I said. "Not really, it's . . ."

"You just said it was."

"Andie doesn't know about him yet, that's all."

Carrie stood up to leave. "Have fun reading your mail."

"Wait a minute. What's this?" I pulled out a letter addressed to Mom.

Carrie noticed the stamp first. "Hong Kong?"

"Hey, look. It's the same handwriting as the Japan letter."

"How can this guy be in so many places at once?" Carrie asked. "Did he sign his name this time?"

I held it up to the window. "Hard to tell. Guess we'll have to wait till Mom comes home."

"Mr. Tate's picking her up from work," Carrie said.

Perfect timing, I thought, snickering.

"I forgot to tell you that Stephanie wants to come stay over here next week," she said, going downstairs.

"Just please keep her out of my room," I hollered down.

On my window seat, I curled up, holding the letter from Lucas Leigh. The seal with the initials was a greenish color this time. Same postmark, though—Cincinnati, Ohio.

I read each word carefully. He liked my story, "Love Times Two," and complimented me on my story line. There was even a separate critique sheet with suggestions for characterization and setting. And he asked my permission to send it to his aunt, Marty Leigh. *I think this story has great possibilities*, he wrote.

Another surprise was he had just purchased a new Corvette. And . . . *gulp!* . . . he was requesting my picture. Could I please send one in my next letter?

I'd have to scrounge to find a picture of myself. One that was recent. One that portrayed maturity, of course.

Gathering up the mail, I carried it down to the kitchen,

placing it on the desk in the corner. A brochure on log homes fell out of the pile. Peeking at it, I shivered as I thought of Mom and Mr. Tate's plans. Quickly, I placed the letter from Hong Kong on top of the stack.

Let's see how Mr. Tate reacts to this, I thought.

In the family room, in search of a picture for Lucas Leigh, I dug out our family photo albums from the large cupboard under the TV. Beginning with last year's school picture, I studied one snapshot after another. There was one of me with my stepbrother, Tyler, on the beach beside the fabulous sand castle we'd made this summer. Another one at Andie's, goofing off in the big tree behind her house. So many to choose from, and none of them right. Convincing Lucas Leigh that I was a woman—which I now was—could be accomplished by the words I chose to write on paper. A visual image might defeat everything I'd tried to do. Unless . . .

A plan . . . to make me look older!

I closed the scrapbook and slid it back into its place in the cupboard. Heading upstairs, I had a fabulous idea. "We're going downtown, Carrie. Come ride bikes with me," I called.

"I'm reading." She was sitting at the kitchen bar with a handful of graham crackers. "Let me finish this chapter."

"Can't. Stores won't be open much longer."

Reluctantly, she closed the book and followed me to the garage, where we hopped on our bikes.

Leading the way, I pedaled down the bricked sidewalk, past the mailbox at the end of our block, through the tree-lined streets to Aspen Street, the main thoroughfare.

Turning left, we raced toward Center Square, a quaint area off the main drag where merchants sold their wares.

The smell of warm cinnamon rolls lured me toward The World's Best Donut Shop. But Lottie's Boutique called silently from two blocks away.

"Where are we going?" Carrie asked, pedaling hard to catch up.

"You'll see." I glanced back at her. Carrie was out of breath trying to match my pace.

"Slow down, Holly," she begged.

"We don't have much time. Lottie's closes at five-thirty."

"I should've stayed home," she complained.

"Mom doesn't want you home alone yet. You're only eight. That's too young to baby-sit yourself."

"I'll be nine next month," she said.

I signaled for a right-hand turn. Carrie did, too.

"We're almost there," I called to her as we rode onto the widened sidewalks of the county courthouse. Clusters of aspen trees grew along the street, framing the area.

"Look, there's Mommy and Mr. Tate," Carrie said, slowing her bike down.

I kept riding. "Where?"

"Coming out of the courthouse, over there."

I braked to slow down, catching a glimpse of them as they walked toward Mr. Tate's car.

"What're they doing?" Carrie asked, waving to them. But they couldn't see us here under the aspen trees. Just as well.

My heart pounded as I stared in disbelief. Couples often got married in front of a judge. Had they united in holy matrimony in some judge's deep, dark chamber?

I watched as Mr. Tate helped Mom into the car, a white

envelope tucked under his arm. Oh no. Had he talked Mom into a quick wedding?

Still, they didn't exactly look like "Just Married" to me. They weren't even holding hands.

I felt like a spy, watching Mr. Tate walk around his car and get in on the driver's side. Inside, he leaned over and gave Mom a peck on the cheek. I could see her buckle her seat belt. If they *were* husband and wife, it didn't look like their marriage was off to a dazzling start. The kind Mom deserved. After all those lonely years without Daddy, working hard at the law firm, never even thinking of dating until a few months ago. Mom deserved a hearts-and-flowers kind of romance.

Wait. . . . Mom wasn't dressed like a bride! She wore a blue-and-white summer suit, her office clothes. No way would Mom get married in *that*.

I felt so confused, I almost turned around and rode home. But I had to check out the wigs at Lottie's Boutique. Lucas Leigh was definitely going to have his picture of me, whether Mom had tied the knot with Mr. Tate or not.

Carrie and I rode side by side in silence. Past the Explore Bookstore. Past Footloose and Fancy Things.

"Stop!" I yelled, backing up.

Carrie hit her brakes. "What's wrong?" she asked.

"Nothing." I pushed the kickstand down. "Check out those shorts and tops to match. That's exactly what I need for tomorrow." I gazed at the cute pink outfit. "I *have* to see it up close. Stay here, Carrie, and watch our bikes," I said.

According to Andie, Danny really liked me. If that was true, I wanted to look extra special for him.

Skipping into the shop, I asked the sales clerk how much for the outfit in the window.

"It's on sale for $49.95," she said, pointing to the mannequin.

My heart sank. I had $65.50 in my savings account. How could I afford both the outfit *and* a wig?

"Thanks anyway," I said, turning to go. Now I had to choose between the new outfit for practicing volleyball with Danny Myers and a wig to make me look older for a photo to impress Lucas Leigh.

"Well, how much?" Carrie asked when I emerged from the shop.

"Too much," I said, getting back on my bike and pedaling fast.

We arrived in front of Lottie's Boutique with only ten minutes to closing.

"What are we doing *here*?" Carrie asked.

"Window shopping," I said, concentrating on the short brunette wig in the corner of the window.

"For wigs?"

"Uh-huh," I said, trying to imagine myself as a brunette.

"Who needs a dumb thing like that?"

Without thinking I said, "Mr. Tate."

Carrie giggled. "No, he doesn't. He'd look real funny with hair."

"It's a thought," I said, laughing.

Lottie's Boutique wasn't exactly hopping with customers. There was only one patron in the store, and she was trying on a blond wig. When she turned to admire it in the mirror, I recognized her. It was Danny's mom!

She recognized me, too. "Hi, Holly," she said, waving.

"Hello, Mrs. Myers," I said, eyeing the wig. "You look pretty as a blonde."

"Well, thank you." She beamed. "If I were twenty years younger, I'd buy a blond fall down to my waist, like *your* hair. Now, *that's* pretty."

I could feel my face growing warm. "Thanks."

"Danny says you hope to make the girls' volleyball team."

I nodded.

"He tells me you're a natural at sports."

"He does?" She was so easy to talk to. Like Danny.

"Yes, and he says you're a writer. Maybe you can tell me more about that tomorrow."

"Tomorrow?"

"Danny wants to bring you over for refreshments after practice at school. Is that okay with you?"

"That sounds nice," I said.

Nice? It was perfectly fabulous!

She studied the wig in the window. "Do you like this one?" she asked, coming near the showcase.

"It looks great on the model, but I doubt it's my style," I said.

"Well, you won't know unless you try it," she said, motioning for the sales clerk.

Before I knew it, I was wearing the wig. Mrs. Myers held up two mirrors behind my head. "Simply lovely," she said.

I moved my head around, examining all sides of the new me. "I, uh, I don't know. The color makes my face look pale."

"And older, too," the clerk said.

Mrs. Myers agreed. "You could get the same look with your *own* hair," she said. "A simple French twist is easy enough."

"Really?" I said. "It's easy?"

"If you'd like, I'll show you tomorrow," Mrs. Myers said.

In the mirrors, I saw Carrie standing behind me. She'd abandoned the bikes and followed me inside. Picking up a short, curly wig, she held it high. "Here," she said. "This one's perfect for Mr. Tate."

Danny's mom nodded, smiling. "I hear congratulations are in order for you girls."

Carrie piped up. "They are?"

"I saw your mother and Mike Tate at the courthouse this afternoon. They said they were picking up a marriage license."

Carrie pulled the wig on, her own long hair hanging down out of it. The news hadn't fazed her one bit.

For me, this bit of news meant hope. After all, a marriage license wasn't a marriage. Besides that, it was good only for thirty days.

10

Mr. Tate was waiting as Carrie and I rode our bikes into the garage. "Your mother's ready to dish up supper," he said sternly, moving Carrie's bike away from Mom's car.

"It was Holly's idea to go downtown," Carrie volunteered.

Just great . . . blame me, I thought.

Mr. Tate stared, no . . . he actually glared at me. "Holly, you're in charge of things while your mother's at work. I'm quite sure you know when suppertime is around here." He checked his watch.

There was no use arguing. Obviously, the man couldn't remember having been a kid. Ever!

Yet he waited for my answer. Finally I said, "I'm sorry, it won't happen again."

"Well, I should hope not," he said. "As soon as your mother and I are married, she'll be here, *at home,* for you children. Now, before you do anything, you must apologize to her."

Must . . . should. This routine was too harsh. On top of that, Mr. Tate never cracked a smile. Was life so serious he couldn't enjoy living? And what was this about Mom quitting work? Wasn't that *her* decision?

Going inside, I washed up, thinking how to apologize to Mom.

A dark cloud hung over me at supper as Mr. Tate announced his wedding plans to my mother. Zach sat beside her while his father did all the talking. I noticed Mom's ring finger was still bare. No sparkling diamond ring.

After supper, when Mr. Tate went into the living room to read the paper, I told Mom I was sorry about being late.

"No problem," she said.

Surprised, I asked, "Did Mr. Tate talk to you about me being late for supper?"

"Not exactly," she said, helping Carrie clear the table. "But Mike's a stickler for promptness."

No kidding.

"Did you see the letter from Hong Kong?" I changed the subject. "Carrie and I are dying to know if it was signed." I put the leftovers away.

"No, as a matter of fact, it isn't," she said. "Which is strange."

I was more curious than ever, but I kept quiet.

"There's another joke in the letter," she said, looking for it on the desk nearby. "Here, listen to this. 'What did the worker bee say to the queen bee?' "

"I give up," I said. "What?"

Mom walked to the sink as she read, " 'Good day, your honeyness.' "

I laughed. "Why would someone write a joke about bees? Does this guy know you and Mr. Tate want to keep bees?"

"I have no idea," Mom said. "It's uncanny."

Carrie seemed to be enjoying this. "And so spooky," she said.

"And there's more," Mom continued. "The writer of the letter says not to worry. He wants to make sure there are many more happy times around here."

"What's *that* supposed to mean?" I asked, eager for another laugh about now.

"How would I know?" Mom said, a frown on her face.

Carrie wiped the table. "*I'll* be happy if Stephanie can come over all next week. Please, can she, Mommy?"

Mr. Tate appeared out of nowhere. "Don't beg your mother, Carrie. The question has already been settled."

This news brought a smile to Carrie's face. So Stephie must be coming to stay with us.

When I hung up the dish towel, I noticed Mom held the mysterious letter behind her back. "Time for family devotions," she announced.

Zach, Carrie, and I followed Mr. Tate downstairs to the family room, like mice following the Pied Piper. Mom came down a few minutes later and sat beside Zachary.

The Scripture was from Romans 1, about encouraging each other in the faith. I listened as Mr. Tate read the devotional book. The story was almost humorous, especially because *he* was the person reading it.

The story was about a boy who complained and criticized his best friend, hoping to get him to do things his way: "Give your friend ten compliments for each negative thing you say to him," the boy's mother suggested. Sadly enough, he couldn't think of that many good things.

My mind wandered, creating an instant list of negative things about Mr. Tate. Could I come up with ten *compliments* for him?

Mr. Tate wrapped things up with a long prayer. He prayed for every missionary I'd ever heard of, and some I hadn't. I really wanted him to pray and ask if God's blessing was on his and Mom's wedding plans. Seemed to me the blessing was definitely missing.

After the prayer Carrie and Zach sat at the computer and played one of our family computer games. I ran upstairs, heading for my room. On the way, I spied Mom's letter from Hong Kong sticking out of the phone book on the kitchen desk. That's when my idea struck.

Disregarding Mom's plea to keep the letter a secret, I went back to the family room and waved the letter in Carrie's face. "Look, Mom opened her letter from Hong Kong," I said, hoping to attract Mr. Tate's attention.

Mom's eyes widened. She leaned forward on the sectional.

Carrie wore a glazed expression as she maneuvered the buttons on the game pad. "Move! You're messing me up," she said.

Even though Carrie wasn't interested, Mr. Tate watched my every move. *Perfect.* This charade wasn't for Carrie's benefit anyhow.

"C'mon, Carrie," I begged, standing between her and the screen. "You *have* to read this letter from Mom's secret admirer."

She pressed the pause button. "Did he sign it this time?" she asked.

"No, but the letter is handwritten, and he seems to think he can make Mom smile again."

Mr. Tate stood up abruptly. "Let me see that letter," he demanded, his hand outstretched.

I glanced at Mom, who was by now in third-degree

agony. Her eyes warned me severely, but I ignored them. Instead I looked Mr. Tate square in the face. "Better ask Mom about it first," I said, playacting for all it was worth.

Mr. Tate looked ridiculous standing in the middle of the family room with his hand reaching out for the letter.

"Mom?" I said, enjoying this repeat performance.

She kicked off her shoes. "Mike, it's nothing, really. Most likely some practical joke. That's all."

I tossed the letter to Mom. She could decide what to do now that Mr. Tate knew a second letter had arrived.

Mission accomplished!

"I think you'd better go to your room, Holly," Mr. Tate ordered.

Mom looked surprised. "Why, Mike? What's the problem?"

He cleared his throat. "You and I need to . . . uh, discuss some things, I believe. Privately." The man was a drill sergeant.

"I'll go," I said. "Gladly."

Tingling with victory, I headed for my room. Now to make my list of ten Tate things, minus the compliments, of course.

I wrote:

Mr. Tate is:
1. Bossy
2. Unreasonable
3. Too strict
4. Bald
5. Too serious
6. Too old (for Mom)
7. Unromantic
8. Stingy (not even a diamond chip for a ring!)

    9. Strange (honeycombs for dessert? Give me a
       break!)
   10. Pushy

With a flick of my wrist, I folded the list and hid it in my bottom drawer. There. I felt better with that out of my system.

Now for something *really* interesting. I found Lucas Leigh's last letter and reread it. His idea about showing my short story to his aunt, Marty Leigh, thrilled me. If the best mystery writer in the world thought I had promise as a writer, I'd definitely believe it.

I read the part where Lucas requested a picture of me. Getting off the floor, I posed for the mirror. I swept my hair up, away from my face, like Danny's mother had suggested.

She was absolutely right. I *did* look older with my long hair up. Forget the wig. I would spend my money on the snappy pink shorts outfit. First thing tomorrow. That is, if Mom let me. No way would she stand for ignoring her wishes about the latest mystery letter. The worst thing she could possibly do was ground me tomorrow. Poor timing on my part. If I didn't show up at the school gym by two o'clock tomorrow, Danny and I could be history! And Kayla would have her man.

♥   ♥   ♥

Early the next morning, my alarm jangled me awake. I stumbled out of bed and hurried to the shower, anxious for my afternoon practice session with Danny. But first—this morning sometime—I planned to stop at Footloose and

Fancy Things and buy the cute outfit in the window.

Pulling on some jeans and a T-shirt, I stumbled back to my room. There sat Mom on my bed. Her eyes were sleepy, but not squinty. "You're up early, Holly."

"I'm going downtown," I said, hoping she'd skip the questions.

"Shopping?"

"Just a little."

"That's something you and I need to do before school starts. Can we set aside some time, just the two of us?"

I liked what I was hearing, but I was puzzled with this no-lecture routine. "Cool," I said, towel-drying my hair.

"Honey," she said slowly. "Who do *you* think is sending those letters to me?"

I perched on my window seat, thinking. "Are you saying you *don't* think it's a practical joke? You only said that to make Mr. Tate think . . ."

"Please don't bring Mike into this," she said, her eyes narrowing into a squint.

"I don't get it, Mom. Why's he so touchy? It's just a letter. Besides, you're not *really* engaged, are you?" I stared at her ring finger.

She touched my comforter lightly, tracing the stitching. "We had a slight disagreement last night," she said softly.

Yes, the beginning of the end! I thought.

"Are you okay, Mom? Did he say something to hurt you?"

"I'm not in the mood to talk about this," she said, getting up. "But I do love you, Holly-Heart. It's been so long since we've had a talk." She looked gloomy now.

"Are you sad about Mr. Tate?" I asked.

"I'm not sad at all. Just missing the way things used to be before . . ."

"Please don't marry him!" I blurted out. "He's not right for us. I know it."

"I have to think things through," she said. "He and I are going to talk on Tuesday night. Will you watch Carrie and Stephie for a few hours then?"

"Sure, Mom," I said, even though I didn't want to make it easy for her to see Mr. Tate again.

"Thanks, sweetie."

"Love you, Mom." I fluffed my hair to dry it.

"Need a ride downtown?" she asked.

I grinned. "Sure, but I have to make a quick stop at the bank as soon as it opens. There's a really cute outfit at Footloose and Fancy Things. You won't believe how cool it is."

Mom's eyes twinkled. "Danny Myers must be someone extra special. When do I get to meet him?"

"You did, sort of. Last year at choir auditions, remember?"

She paused to think. "Is he tall with auburn hair?"

"And an amazing memory. Danny remembers everything—even my favorite soda. You should hear him quote entire chapters from the Bible. And he prays over his meals. Even at school."

"This boy sounds too good to be true," she said with a sad little smile. She headed toward her room.

I prayed silently that someone like Danny would sneak into Mom's life. The anonymous letter writer was right. Mom *did* need to laugh again.

♥ ♥ ♥

By the time we finished eating breakfast, it was time to leave for the bank. Carrie and I climbed into the car, and I thought how fabulous it was being with Mom again, alone, without Mr. Tate hovering endlessly.

Mom and Carrie stayed in the car while I ran into the bank and withdrew fifty-five dollars from my account. I figured with tax, I'd need extra for the expensive outfit.

Soon enough I was carrying the two-piece outfit to the car, swinging the bag as I bounced down the steps. I showed it off to Carrie and Mom as we rode home.

"It's definitely your color," Mom said with an approving glance. "I hope you tried it on."

"Don't worry. I've had enough outfits that were too loose around my waist not to remember."

Carrie piped up, "You don't look *that* skinny anymore, Holly."

Mom shot me a knowing look. "You're filling out, all right. And it's all happened this summer."

"Maybe my sister will get fat," Carrie said, giggling.

Mom turned into the driveway. "That'll be the day," she said, turning off the ignition.

I spied the mail truck coming. Carrie saw it, too. "Beat you to the mailbox," I challenged her, running toward it.

I won. Reaching for the mail, I immediately saw a letter addressed to Mom. It was postmarked Hawaii. I studied the envelope. "Hey, check this out." I showed the letter to Carrie. "There's no return address."

"Is it from the same guy?" she asked, peering at the handwriting.

"How can it be? It's Hawaii. Besides, the handwriting is different." I hurried up the steps and into the house.

Carrie ran ahead of me into the kitchen. "Holly's got the mail," she called to Mom.

"Thanks," Mom said, spying the letter. "Hmm, who's this from?" Quickly, she tore open the envelope.

I leaned against Mom, following along as she read silently.

> *Dear Susan,*
>   *Need another laugh? Here's a silly riddle to brighten your day: "What did the queen bee say to the baby bee?*
>   *"Bee-hive yourself!"*
>   *I simply couldn't resist this bee joke. It's so dumb, it's funny. Can't quite imagine you getting close to a beehive, let alone gathering the honey.*
>   *With sweet thoughts of you,*
>   *Your Secret Admirer*

"This is nuts," Carrie said. "Who *is* this guy going around the world writing letters to our mom?"

"He certainly knows a lot about me," Mom said, sitting at the bar and reading the letter again.

I grabbed her arm. "Isn't this exciting?"

"Either exciting or a sick joke," she said.

"Any idea who's writing to you?" I said.

"Didn't I ask *you* the same question just this morning?" She planted her elbows on the bar.

Pulling out a stool, I hoisted myself up. "You don't think *I* put someone up to this, do you?"

Mom tapped her pink fingernails on the counter top. "This is just so . . . bizarre."

"And mysterious," Carrie chimed in.

"And now *two* different handwritings," Mom said, frowning.

"How could someone possibly know all this stuff about us, er . . . you?" I asked, feeling uneasy, like someone might be spying on us.

"I don't know, but I'd like to find out." A hint of a smile crossed her face. "You are not to mention *this* letter to Mike, uh, Mr. Tate," she said. "Do you understand, girls?"

"Yes," I said.

"Promise?"

I looked into her blue eyes. "I promise."

She pulled Carrie over next to her. "And you?"

"I promise," Carrie said solemnly.

"I mean it." She shook her finger at us.

The tone of her voice and her eyes indicated she meant business like never before. However, there was one minor detail Mom had overlooked. Stephanie was coming over tomorrow night. What if *she* happened to spill the beans to Mr. Tate on Tuesday when he came to pick up Mom?

The more I thought about my nosy little cousin hanging out at our house, the better I liked it. The setup was fabulous.

Mom fixed cheeseburgers for lunch. I ate hurriedly, then excused myself. There were many advantages to not having Mr. Tate around. *He* wouldn't approve of eating and running. Mom was cool. She didn't mind as long as I didn't rush though supper, our special family time.

"Spaghetti tonight," she called as I took the steps two at a time.

In my room, I brushed back my hair, pulling it into a single ponytail. Next came the new shorts outfit. A perfect fit! I squirted on some perfume, wondering if my cheeks needed a touch of blush. Nah, I thought, looking in the mirror. I was still rosy-tan from the summer.

I did take a minute to apply the light brown mascara Mom let me wear. One final look told me I was ready to meet Danny Myers.

11

On my way to the school, I wondered how it would feel when Danny told me whatever was on his mind.

"He likes you," Andie had insisted to me.

Giddy with excitement, I imagined how the volleyball practice session might turn out. I sped up my pace, hurrying down the street to the school.

As usual, Danny was prompt. He met me at the gym, wearing green gym shorts and a white T-shirt. The contrast of white against his face made him look tanner than usual. "Hey! Ready to warm up?"

"Okay, let's go," I said, following him around the gym. A believer in limbering up the muscles before working out, Danny put me through my paces, showing me how to stretch out properly so I wouldn't strain any muscles.

Next he had me practice serving techniques—how to put a spin on a fast serve. We bumped the ball, spiked the ball, and set it up. But I could think of only one thing: When would Danny reveal his romantic interest in me?

Thirsty from running around, I stopped at the drinking fountain. Danny came over and got a drink, too. But he remained silent about anything but volleyball.

Over an hour later, Danny stopped bouncing the ball and held it. "I think that's enough for today." He flashed me a grin. "You're great, Holly. I hope you'll make the team."

"Thanks." Still panting from the exercise, I wiped my face.

"Want to drop by my house for a snack?" he asked. "My mom's expecting you."

"Okay." I could only hope his mom hadn't said anything about seeing me at the wig shop yesterday.

Danny and I began walking the long trek to his house. He lived at least a mile from the school. Now maybe we'd have time to talk for a change. Really talk.

"My mom baked your favorite cake." His eyes twinkled.

"How'd she know?"

"*I* remembered," he said.

My heart pumped ninety miles an hour. "Oh yeah, I should've *remembered* you would remember." With that we burst into laughter. Danny's green eyes danced in the afternoon light.

We walked in silence for another half block. *What is he waiting for? What if Andie's wrong?* I thought.

At last I broke the silence. "Do you really think I have a chance of making the team?"

"We'll keep working at it," he said. The way he said *we'll* made my heart skip a beat. That is until he suggested that maybe Kayla Miller could be of some assistance, too.

"I'm fine with *you*," I said, hoping he'd take the hint.

Instead he asked about my short stories. An awkward change of topics.

"Oh, I love to write mysteries. But they're not so easy,"

I replied. "You have to know the ending so you can work the plot backward."

"That's good. I'll remember that," he said, smiling.

Good for you, I thought, totally confused.

♥ ♥ ♥

Danny's mom had ice-cold lemonade and angel food cake waiting in the breakfast nook for us when we arrived. What an inviting sight after the long walk in the hot sun.

"Did you have a good time?" she asked, pouring lemonade.

Danny nodded, smiling. "Holly's something else. You should see her catch on . . . and fast."

I honestly wanted to believe him. He sounded convincing. But I guess I wanted more than compliments. If only Andie hadn't said anything.

Mrs. Myers sat at the table with us. She opened her address book and found the M's. "What's your street address, Holly?"

I must've looked puzzled at first.

"I like to keep a record of addresses of Danny's friends, you know, for party invitations, things like that," she said.

"It's 207 Downhill Court," I replied quickly, observing the graceful motion of her hand. "You write something like my aunt Marla. She had the most beautiful handwriting ever."

"Mom's been writing like that all her life," Danny joked.

"I'm not kidding, Danny. Look at it . . . her handwriting's beautiful. Those perfectly formed loops on her Ls and the Ts are crossed slightly above the center of the line. Wow."

"Which tells something about Mom's personality," Danny said. "If I remember correctly, the loops mean she has confidence and self-discipline, which is true."

I looked at him curiously. "Do you know about handwriting analysis?"

"Sure . . . there's a book on handwriting at the library. I read it a couple of years ago. Let me think a minute." He stared into space a second. I could almost hear his brain sorting through one memory bank after another. "Yes, there it is."

"Where?" I said, looking around the breakfast nook.

His mom chuckled along with me. "Danny's amazing," she said, excusing herself while I waited for the final "read out" from my friend's wonder-brain.

At last he snapped his fingers. "I've got it! The book I read is called *Handwriting: A Key to the Real You.*"

Faster than a speeding microchip, I thought of Mom's mysterious letters. The handwriting had changed, though. The first two letters had definitely been scrawled. Today's letter was more refined, almost stylish. Had the letters been written by two different men?

"Danny." I turned to him suddenly, filling him in on the strange letters Mom was getting in the mail. "Want to help me solve an international mystery?"

"What are the clues?"

"I'll make a list for you," I said.

Eagerly, Danny went to the kitchen counter, pulling out scraps of paper from the top drawer. "Here's some paper." He brought the tablet to me and scooted it across the table.

I began to outline everything I could remember about

the letters and their content, showing Danny when I finished. "There. Any ideas how to tell who's writing anonymous letters to my mom?"

"We could check out the handwriting book at the library," he said. "We'll study the penmanship on the envelope and in the letters to see what personality type we're dealing with. It should eventually lead you to your mystery man."

"That's logical," I said.

Logic . . . Danny's strongest point.

Mrs. Myers peeked around the corner. "Holly? Any time you're ready for your new hairdo, let me know."

"I almost forgot," I said, studying the list of clues once more.

Danny looked startled. "You're not going to cut her hair, are you, Mom?" he asked, desperation in his voice.

"Never," she said, waving her well-manicured hand.

Danny seemed to admire my hair with a fleeting glance. Hmm, maybe Danny wasn't all logic after all. . . .

"Why is my mom changing your hair?" he asked pointedly.

"I want a new look, and your mom's the pro," I said, determining to conceal the real reason. (Lucas Leigh, the secret *older* man in my life.)

Danny said no more about my new do, gathering up the notes I'd written.

His mom directed me to the powder room off the kitchen. In the mirror, I observed her every move as she wrapped my hair into a smooth French twist, securing it with thin hairpins.

Stepping back when she was finished, I stared at the young woman in the mirror. "It's so . . . well, grown-up!"

"It certainly is. And quite becoming, too," she said.

I touched my hair lightly. "Do you mind if I wear it this way home? I'll return the pins."

"Go ahead, have fun with it. And forget the pins. They're yours to keep."

"Thanks, Mrs. Myers," I said, feeling shy.

"Call me Ruthanne," she said with a broad smile.

I nodded, feeling uneasy about addressing a grown-up that way. She pointed me in the direction of the family room, where Danny sat waiting with his back to us.

I stepped into the hall, inching my way toward him. I called, "Guess who?"

He turned slowly, tilting his head.

I stood very still. "It's the new me. Like it?"

He blinked his eyes. "You look eighteen, at least."

"Really? *That* old?"

"It's incredible, Holly."

I couldn't let on how pleased I was with my advanced age. "Guess I'd better head home," I said, noticing the clock on the mantel. It was nearly five o'clock.

Danny seemed confused. "You're going out in public like that?"

"Why not?"

"It, uh . . . it's not you," he stuttered.

"Well, yes, it *is* me," I said, beginning to feel frustrated. Was he ever going to talk to me about, well, whatever Andie thought he had on his mind, and possibly in his heart, too?

"We can ride home on the bus, okay?" Danny suggested.

"Sure," I said.

I thanked Mrs. Myers repeatedly for the new hairdo and

refreshments. Then the shyest, most logical guy in Dressel Hills and the amazing new Holly Meredith walked together to the city bus stop.

♥   ♥   ♥

Downtown, sitting side by side in the bus waiting for the light to change, I noticed a photo booth in the drug-store window across the street. "Let's get off here," I said, pulling the cord overhead.

"Where are you going?" he asked, catching up with me.

I held my hands up to protect my hairdo from the evening breeze. "I want to take a picture of my new look," I said, depositing the coins in the slot outside the mini photo booth.

Parting the purple curtain, I sat down and posed. First, two serious shots, then two smiley ones. Still seeing spots, I stepped out of my private photo shoot feeling like a movie actress. I waited for the pictures to develop, frustrated by Danny's restlessness.

"They'll be ready in a second," I said, thinking about Lucas and hoping one of these was good enough to send off to him. If I mailed it before six o'clock tonight, he'd have my picture by next Tuesday.

All four poses turned out great. I was delighted. Only *one* pose was suitable for Lucas Leigh, however. I could hardly believe it was me. And neither could Danny.

"It's a sophisticated side of you I've never seen before," he said.

"And might never see again," I teased.

"May I have one of those?" he asked, studying the pictures.

"Sure. Which one?"

He pointed to the very one I planned to send to Lucas.

12

I stalled about the photos, talking Danny into letting me show them to Mom first. Then we caught the bus again, riding it to Downhill Court.

"See you in church tomorrow?" Danny asked as the bus stopped to let off passengers one block before my street.

"Sure," I said. "And thanks for your help at the gym today."

The bus jolted to a stop at the corner of Aspen and Downhill Court. "You'll make the team if you keep practicing," he said as we hopped off.

"Hope so." We crossed the street, the sun beginning to drop behind the mountains.

"I'll call you, Holly." He walked me to the door.

"Okay."

He opened the door for me. "Maybe my parents could invite you and your mom and sister over sometime . . . to get better acquainted. Since we go to the same church, you know."

"Really?" I said, not sure that Mom would approve. But then it wasn't like Danny and I were actually dating or anything. Shoot, he hadn't even said he liked me yet.

"Well, I'll see you tomorrow, Holly-Heart."

I blushed. "That's my mom's nickname for me."

"Mind if *I* call you that?"

"Better ask Mom," I teased.

"Okay." He waved as he turned to leave.

I dashed into the house, conscious of simmering spaghetti sauce. The aroma filled the house.

Upstairs, I yanked the bottom drawer of my bureau open, finding my letter to Lucas Leigh. I searched for an envelope and a scissors to cut the best picture off the strip of four. Carefully examining the pose one last time, I slipped it into the envelope.

"I need a stamp quick," I called to Mom as I raced downstairs.

"Kitchen desk drawer, top right," she said, stirring the sauce, her back to me.

I snatched up a self-stick stamp and plopped it on the envelope. "I'll be right back." I glanced at the clock. Ten minutes till six o'clock!

"Holly," Mom called to me when I was halfway out the back door. "Andie has been trying to reach you all afternoon. I said you'd call her the minute you got home."

"Can't *this* minute," I shouted back. "I have to catch the last mail pickup." With that I rushed down the back steps, my tennies flying over the bricked sidewalk to the mailbox on the corner.

Just ahead of me, I could see the mail truck making its turn onto my street. I ran faster. The key dangled on the postman's chain as he reached to unlock the mail receptacle. Out of breath, I sprinted toward him.

"Looks like you're just in time, missy." He reached for my letter.

"Wait a sec," I said, checking to see if everything was in place.

"Take your time." He scooped up a pile of mail and headed for the postal truck.

Then I did a strange thing. I held the envelope close to my heart and made a wish. . . . And I whispered, "Please, make this wish come true."

Slam-a-clump! The mail truck door shut. The uniformed postal worker climbed behind the steering wheel.

"Here's my letter," I said, slipping it into his hand.

With a wave, he was off.

I stood there a moment, watching as the truck made its way down the tree-lined street, wondering what had come over me. Making wishes was for blowing out candles on your birthday. Not for mailing letters to secret pen pals!

Turning, I plodded back toward the house. When I strolled in the back door, Mom mentioned that Andie had called again. Inquisitive Andie. She would want to hear how things went with Danny, of course.

Well, there was nothing to tell. Except he *did* call me *Holly-Heart* and asked for my picture! And he said he'd see me tomorrow at church . . . *and* there was the possible invitation to his house. Replaying the events of the day, I realized there might be some good stuff to share with my best friend. Just not earthshaking stuff like she'd said there would be.

My thoughts strayed to Lucas. Now, *there* was a man who wasn't afraid to speak his mind. Sensitive, too. But then, writers were like that.

Reading Lucas's letters made me giddy, even though he

lived far away in Ohio. Danny, on the other hand, lived across town. Yet sometimes he seemed out of reach, even though I was pretty sure he liked me. Standing in the kitchen, I was completely confused.

"Wash up for supper, girls," Mom said. Looking at me for the first time, she did a double take. "What happened to your hair?"

I grinned at her. "It's the new me." I turned around, showing off. "Like it?"

The phone rang.

Mom waved her hand. "It's probably Andie again. Let it ring till after supper."

Hearing the phone *ring-ringing* and ignoring it was like Mom stashing strawberry ice cream in a padlocked freezer and throwing away the key. Pure torture.

♥   ♥   ♥

After supper, I deserted the kitchen to call Andie back. Taking the phone downstairs into my "office," I sat on the lid of the toilet seat and phoned Andie.

She answered the phone like this: "Okay, let's have it. Everything from the very first second."

"Well, hello to you, too," I said, laughing.

"I'm waiting," came her no-nonsense reply.

"Okay," I said. "Danny met me at the school gym, wearing green shorts and a T-shirt. There was a pocket on the left side of the shirt with blue stitching and—"

"Holly, get real. Who cares about topstitching? Get to the good stuff."

"Like what?"

"C'mon. When did he tell you, well, you know? Did you hold hands or anything?"

"Nothing like that happened," I said. "You must be dreaming. Danny never even mentioned it."

"He didn't? But Billy said—"

"Look, Andie, I'm not interested in your secondhand information. Danny can talk to *me*. I don't want to hear things passed from Billy to you . . . to me."

"Hey, don't get huffy," she said. "I just thought—"

"Yeah, well, you *thought* wrong."

"It's not my fault," she insisted. "Billy told me exactly what Danny told him."

"And I'm not playing Whisper Down the Lane, either. Besides, I have a much more *mature* relationship going on right now."

Andie was silent, but only for a half second. "What are you saying?"

"I'm talking about Lucas Leigh. He's a junior in college this year and he just bought a new Corvette."

"So where are you hiding him?" Andie asked.

"In Ohio."

"Where'd you meet him?"

"I didn't." I had to laugh. "He's one of my pen pals."

"How come *I* wasn't informed of this?"

"I've been keeping Lucas a secret on purpose. I don't know why. Maybe just for the fun of it."

"Or maybe," she added, "to win our pen pal contest by cheating. You're supposed to report all pen pals by Labor Day, the day before school starts. That's only two weeks away."

"Well, I'm reporting *now*. It's not Labor Day yet, is it?"

"I'm still winning," she bragged. "I got two more names

from the Philippines just today."

"Okay, let's just say you won," I said. "I don't care about this stupid contest anymore. It's more fun having just a couple of dependable pen pals, and one to exchange manuscripts with."

"What?" she gasped.

"You heard me. Lucas and I are critiquing each other's writing. It's very exciting."

"Sounds boring, if you ask me."

"Boring to someone who doesn't write stories or keep a journal."

"You don't know if I write in one or not," she shot back. "Maybe I do, maybe I don't. You'd better watch out, Holly, I could drop this news about Lucas Leigh to Billy and he might—"

"Sounds like blackmail to me," I said. "We're best friends, remember?"

"Whatever," she said snidely. "This conversation's going nowhere."

"You got *that* right. Call me when you're thinking clearly. Good-bye." I hung up.

♥ ♥ ♥

In church the next day, Mom sat with Carrie and me, minus Mr. Tate. *He* sat three rows ahead of us with Zachary, who kept waving his Sunday school paper back at Mom.

Across the aisle, Andie was sitting with Billy Hill and gloating about it when I caught her gaze. Danny was sandwiched in between his own parents, like it was the safest place to be, with Kayla Miller sitting directly behind him.

And Paula Miller was perched beside Jared Wilkins, who wore a satisfied grin.

I imagined Lucas Leigh escorting me to the church pew, holding the hymnal during the songs, and putting a wad of money into the offering plate.

After church, Danny motioned to me. I told Mom I'd meet her at the car.

"That's her boyfriend," Carrie said, making kissing sounds with her lips.

I ignored her and hurried over to see Danny. Kayla waited in the side aisle, probably hoping to talk to him.

"Hey, Holly," he said. "Your hair looks much better today."

"Thanks," I said, touching it.

"Will you be home this afternoon?" he asked.

"Sure."

"Great. I'll give you a call, and maybe we can go to the library to look for that handwriting book. Okay with you?"

Seeing him still made my heart pound. "Good idea," I said brightly, hoping to discourage Kayla, who was still hanging around.

"What did your mom think of the pictures?" he asked.

"Pictures? Oh, those," I said, remembering fast. "Haven't had a chance to show them yet. But Mom really liked my hair up."

His parents waved to him from the back of the church.

"I think my dad's anxious for dinner," he said. "I'll call you around three o'clock."

"Okay. Bye," I said, waving triumphantly to Kayla, who spun away when she heard Danny say he planned to call me later.

On my way out, I noticed Mr. Tate. He nodded, and I

smiled without speaking. Seeing him again made me realize how much better off we were without him hanging around.

Back at home, we savored Mom's famous roast and onions, potatoes, and carrots dinner. She sang church songs while carrying serving dishes into the dining room.

Then, after stuffing ourselves, I spooned up the leftovers into plastic containers, thinking of Mom. She seemed much happier again. Back to normal. When Mr. Tate did his "helicopter-hover," she seemed tense. Insecure Mr. Tate had a way of cluttering up the atmosphere.

Wiping the crumbs off the place mats, I struggled with the idea of Mom seeing him again this coming Tuesday night to work things out between them. I wondered how Mr. Tate would react to another letter from Mom's secret admirer. Of course, I wouldn't think of disobeying her *this* time, but as soon as my cousin Stephanie arrived tonight, I'd see about putting her up to something. Anything!

The doorbell rang and I ran to get it.

What was *this*? Through the screen door, I stared down at Zachary Tate. Then I noticed Mr. Tate parking his car in our driveway.

"Hi, Holly," Zach said. "My dad wants to see your mom."

"Oh really," I said. "Does *she* know about this?"

Mom strolled into the living room. "Open the door, Holly-Heart." When she saw Zach, she bent down and held her arms wide.

He ran to her, snuggling against her. "Oh, I've missed my handsome boy," she said.

Mr. Tate was all smiles as he landed his helicopter presence in our living room. "And we've missed you, too," he said, gazing at Mom.

Zach looked up longingly at Mom. Man, it was disgusting. And just when I thought things were falling apart with these people. Guess absence does make strange things happen.

"Zach wants to stay here and play with Carrie. Okay with you, Holly?" Mr. Tate asked.

"Actually, I have plans this afternoon. I mean, I can't baby-sit for you today." I looked at Mom for moral support.

"We wouldn't have to be gone long," Mr. Tate said to Mom. "Wouldn't you like to go for coffee somewhere, Susan?"

"Perhaps for an hour or so." She turned to me. "It won't be baby-sitting for you, not if Zach and Carrie play together. Maybe they could ride bikes while you read or whatever. Isn't Zach's bike still out in the garage?"

The helicopter blades hummed loudly as Mr. Tate landed on Mom's suggestion. "Splendid idea. Yes, by all means, go outdoors with the children, Holly. Get them in shape for roughing it in the mountains." At that he winked at Mom.

I breathed deeply and then said again, "I'm sorry, Mr. Tate, I have plans to go to the library. You should call ahead if you want me to watch Zach. You'll have to take him along with you or else take him home." It felt good finally standing up to Mr. Michael Tate.

Mom looked at me, surprised.

Surprised? Wait a minute, I thought she'd be furious!

Encouraged, I dug my heels in for the fight.

Mr. Tate revved his motor and nearly lifted off the floor with his hovering. "I'm not asking you, Holly, I'm *telling* you. Zachary will stay here with you and Carrie. Now, do as your mother said and get the bikes out of the garage."

I hurried to my mother's side. "Mom," I said, "do I have to change my library plans with Danny?"

She looked at Mr. Tate. "I'm really sorry about this, Mike. Holly does have some very special plans with a friend of hers. And I think she's right, you should call ahead. As for today, I believe I'll be staying home with my daughters."

Now it was Mr. Tate's turn to look shocked. "Don't let Holly run your life, Susan," he retorted. "If she were my daughter I'd—"

"Well, she's *not* your daughter, Mike. Not now or ever. And if you don't mind, I have some important business to take care of." Hastily, she showed the bewildered-looking man to the front door.

Zachary started to cry.

Oh great, I thought. Just when Mom was doing so well and telling it like it is, Zach—the real focus of her affection—was going to get emotional and spoil everything!

"Come here, darling," Mom said, reaching for him. She knelt on the floor and cuddled him. "You're okay. That's right," she said, stroking his hair, rocking back and forth.

"As you know, Zachary is easily upset," Mr. Tate said accusingly. "He'll be fine when we're back home. Come along, Zachary."

"I want to stay here," the boy whined, clinging to Mom. "I want Susan to be my mommy."

Talk about manipulation. Here was a nine-year-old pro.

"I know, I know," said Mom in hushed tones. "We'll have to see about that later."

"I'll call you, Susan," Mr. Tate said, leading Zach out the door.

"No, I'll call *you*," Mom said with determination.

I wanted to cheer as the Tates backed out of the driveway. Inside, a strong feeling told me Mom and Mr. Tate were through. Finished!

13

Deliberately, Mom turned and marched into the kitchen. I wanted to cheer her actions, but I bit my tongue.

At exactly three o'clock the phone rang. It was Danny.

"Hi, Holly-Heart," he said.

I laughed softly. "Did you ask my mom if you could call me that?"

"Is she there?" he asked seriously.

"Danny, how can you be so gullible? Of course you don't have to ask her permission."

"I was just joking," he said, but I wondered if he was saying that to cover up. "I called the library about the handwriting book. It's on reserve in your name. We can pick it up today if you'd like."

"Perfect. Now all I have to do is find Mom's letters so we can compare the handwriting." I walked downstairs with the phone, hoping for some privacy. Carrie was reading on the sofa, so I ducked into the bathroom. "My mom doesn't know anything about what we're up to," I said, lowering my voice. "We have to keep this mystery-solving stuff a secret, okay?"

"That's cool," he said. "But will you be in trouble if she finds out?"

"You know what? I think she'd really like to know who's sending the anonymous letters. And, get this, the last one was signed, 'With sweet thoughts of you.' Isn't that romantic?" I almost forgot I was talking to a boy!

"Wouldn't it be even more romantic if she knew who was writing to her?" he said.

"That's what I'm hoping to figure out. With your help, of course."

Danny was quiet for a moment, then he said, "Holly, are you hoping your mom's secret admirer might qualify for a stepdad?"

"Not exactly. But if Mom's going to have a boyfriend, er, *man* friend, it would be nice if he's someone *I* like, too. And so far, the mystery letter writer beats all the competition to pieces."

"Even better than that nice man with the sick boy?"

"Well, between you and me, Mr. Tate's not so nice. And his son isn't so sick anymore. It's too bad about Zach, though, he would have been a nice stepson for Mom."

"Really?" He seemed surprised.

"Yeah, Mom got attached to him. It all started last spring when she signed up to teach Zach's Sunday school class, then found out he had cancer. This summer he's been around here a lot. Besides, Mom has a soft place in her heart for kids. If she and Daddy had stayed married, there'd probably be a bunch of us by now."

"It's hard for me to imagine brothers and sisters running around everywhere," he said. "Being the only child isn't that bad."

I could tell he wasn't ready for sweet talk on the phone.

Given more time, maybe . . . After all, for two members of the opposite sex, Danny and I were nearly as close as best friends could be—minus the boy-girl stuff.

There was a click, signaling another call.

"Uh, Danny, can you hold a sec?"

"No problem."

I answered the incoming call. "Hello?"

"This must be one of my favorite nieces," said a deep voice.

"Uncle Jack, hi!" I said, excited to hear from him.

"Has Stephanie arrived there yet?" he asked.

"She's coming tonight for supper. You could probably still catch her at the Millers' house."

"Thanks."

"When are *you* coming back to Dressel Hills?" I asked.

"Next week sometime. The boys and I are doing some sight-seeing here in Seattle today before my business meetings start up again."

"Wow, it'll be cool having you and my cousins living so close to us."

"Cool, indeed," he said, chuckling. "See you soon, Holly, dear."

I switched back to the other line. "Danny, are you still there?"

"Uh-huh." He seemed distracted. "I'm making loops."

"You're what?"

"Perfecting my handwriting. Trying to imitate my mother's flawless penmanship."

I filled him in on the other phone call. "That was my uncle Jack calling long distance."

"Isn't he the husband of your favorite aunt? The one who died last year?" asked Danny.

"You remembered?" I was sincerely impressed.

"Of course," Danny said softly. "And I was sorry to hear about it."

"You know, I still miss Aunt Marla. Next to Mom she was the sweetest person I've ever known. She used to wear her hair up sometimes, too," I said. "Oh, tell your mother I really like how she fixed my hair."

"Well, it wasn't *my* favorite," he said. "But come over any time. My mom likes girls, probably because she doesn't have any."

"Maybe she'll have a daughter-in-law someday," I said.

That topic must've made him nervous. He changed the subject instantly. "Can you meet me at the library in thirty minutes?"

"Sure, I'll be there."

"Good-bye, Holly-Heart." The way he said my nickname sent a tingle down my spine.

"Bye," I said.

Carrie was still curled up on the sofa, reading. I darted past her, heading upstairs. On the living room couch, Mom lay sound asleep. I crept over to snoop at a piece of paper lying on her lap.

It was a copy of the contract on the mountain property. Leaning closer, I scanned some of the first paragraphs. Wow, it looked like she *was* getting out of the deal with Mr. Tate. She'd marked out words and initialed everything. More than ever I hoped their short-lived romance was over.

Turning toward the kitchen, I went in search of Mom's secret-admirer letters. The last I'd seen them, they were in the kitchen on the desk. I poked through the bills, separating them from a pile of coupons. I looked under the phone book. No letters.

The next most logical place to look was probably Mom's bedroom. Logical. Was I beginning to think like Danny?

Tiptoeing upstairs to her bedroom, I sneaked across the floor. I spied something colorful sticking out of her Bible on the lamp table beside her bed—the foreign stamps on the envelopes.

"This is not really stealing, Lord," I prayed as I whisked the letters away to my room. "I'm doing this with Mom's best interest in mind, but I'm sure you already know that, right, Lord?"

Curling my legs under me, I snuggled against Bearie-O on my window seat. I'd almost forgotten to thank the Lord for answering my prayer about Mr. Tate and Mom.

Impulsively, I hopped off the seat and rushed to open the bottom dresser drawer. Reaching for my secret prayer list, I found the page with my number-one most urgent request: *Please keep Mom and Mr. Tate from ending up together.* I added the date of the answered prayer: Sunday, August 22.

ONLY GOD COULD DO THIS! I wrote in giant letters.

14

The public library was nearly empty when I arrived. Danny—punctual as always—waved to me from a table near the reference section.

"Hey, Holly. Check this out." He pointed to a page in the handwriting book.

Sitting down, I saw a lineup of famous signatures from George Washington to John Kennedy. And . . . Winston Churchill, Laura Ingalls Wilder, and Billy Graham.

I pulled Mom's letters out of my backpack. "Here's the first one . . . from Japan." I showed him the second letter. "This one has a Hong Kong postmark and stamp, with the same handwriting. Then a third letter came from Hawaii. The writing is different, don't you think?"

He agreed with me, then opened the handwriting book to chapter two. "Let's take a look at the slant of the letters. It says here that if the writing leans to the right, the writer has a strong urge to communicate. In other words, your mom's mystery man is talkative."

We compared the two different handwritings.

"What do you think?" I reached for my tablet.

"We need a list of characteristics for the writer of the first two letters and a separate list for the latest letter writer," Danny said.

"I can do that." I marked my headings on the lined paper. *Writer 1* for the two letters from Asia and *Writer 2* for the letter from Hawaii.

An hour later, the great list maker had two lists—with Danny's help, of course.

WRITER 1	WRITER 2
Left-handed	Communicative
Immature	Fun-loving
Imaginative	Practical joker
Determined	Confident
Brave	Family pride
Arrogant	Intelligent
Sloppy	Trustworthy
Athletic	Athletic
	Business-minded
	Religious
	Romantically inclined

"Hey, I think I like writer number two," I said, studying the two lists. "He's cool."

"Stepfather material?" Danny joked.

"Puh-leez!" I said it too loudly. The librarian raised her dark eyebrows and stared at us like a bull ready to charge.

Just then, out of the shelves behind us, came a mysterious-sounding voice. "Better keep it down over there, or you might end up with the boogeyman's signature."

Startled, I whirled around, catching a glimpse of Jared

Wilkins' brown hair. I'd know those gorgeous locks anywhere—only because I was obsessed with him last year in
seventh grade. Probably still would be, except he was so
immature . . . and such a jerk.

"Who was that?" Danny asked, looking around.

"Just your imagination," I said, laughing.

Now the librarian really did look ready to charge; in
fact, she stood up and leaned against her desk.

"We're going to get kicked out of this place. That's
never happened to me before," Danny said, a worried look
on his face.

"Shh," I said, my finger on my lips.

"Can we please not get thrown out?" he whispered.

"Relax. Don't worry so much. Here," I said, shoving a
blank piece of paper under his nose. "Write your first, middle, and last name."

Danny frowned. "What for?"

"For me to figure *you* out, that's what."

"Oh, *I* get it. You think now that you've seen one book
on the subject, you're a pro at graphology."

"Hey, that's good," I said. "Let your emotions come out
sometimes. It's not good to hold them in so much. Gives
people ulcers."

"I already have one," he said so straight-faced I be-
lieved him.

"I'm sorry. I didn't know." Once again, I spotted Jared
sneaking around behind the shelves, holding his hand over
his mouth to cover his laughter. While Danny studied our
list, I shook my head at Jared. It was a warning for him to
get lost. Fast!

I should've known he would ignore my signal. Here he

came, wearing jeans and jacket to match, rolled up at the sleeves.

"Hello, Holly Meredith," he crooned, soft enough to keep us from getting booted out.

Danny looked up. "Doing research today?"

Jared smiled flirtatiously at me. "You might say that."

I couldn't help it; I blushed.

Danny sat up straight in his chair. "Ready for track season?" he asked.

"Always," Jared said, flexing his arm muscles. "Well, it looks like you two have some work to finish. Catch you later." He swaggered past the librarian, who seemed to be holding back her urge to charge us . . . and not for overdue books, either.

"Let's review all the angles," Danny said, "and take a look at the content of the letters."

I pushed Jared Wilkins out of my mind as we reviewed the silly riddles about the bald man without any locks, the "your honeyness" queen bee, and the beehive.

"It appears someone knows your mother was dating that Tate fellow and hoped to divert her attention," Danny said.

"Makes sense."

"Here's something." He pointed at the first letters. "It looks like a young person started writing the letters and then someone with 'family pride'—that could be a father or an older friend—took over the writing."

"According to our lists, these two writers have something in common. Athletic ability," I said, rechecking.

"Now think, Holly. Who do you know that's left-handed, has a great imagination, isn't afraid to take risks, and plays sports?"

I kept staring at the list. "And he must have a messy room and think he's hot stuff."

Danny leaned closer, elbows on the table, resting his chin on his fists.

"Only one person fits that description," I said after a long moment. "My cousin Stan."

"Who?"

"My fifteen-year-old schizoid cousin. Uncle Jack's son."

"Are you sure?" Danny asked, his eyes searching mine.

"I'm positive."

Just then I noticed Kayla Miller crouching down, pretending to look at the bottom shelf in one of the reference sections. No way did I want her in on this secret mission. Quickly, I gathered up our notes. "I need some fresh air," I said.

Danny followed, checking out the handwriting book, asking for my card as we arrived at the bullpen, er, checkout desk.

"Keep those lists handy," he said as we headed into the bright Colorado sun.

It was fabulously hot for late August. As we passed the city park, near the library, I noticed the sky was cloudless. Families were gathered for picnics under stately cottonwood trees, enjoying the last days before school doors opened.

My mind zoomed back to my oldest cousin. Why would Stan write those stupid letters to Mom? And what was he doing in Japan? I knew he had gone along on a business trip with Uncle Jack, but I'd never heard they were going overseas. And what older buddy did he know in Hawaii who could have been bribed to write the latest letter?

I studied the list for writer number two as we strolled

through the grounds near the courtyard. "This writer is talkative, has a great sense of humor, would write an anonymous letter as a joke, and takes pride in his family," I said, thinking out loud.

Danny continued, "And he must have kids, or else he's proud of his own parents."

"Good point." I sat on the concrete strip that ran along the front of the county courthouse grounds.

"If he's religious, that might mean he's a Christian," Danny remarked. "*That's* good."

"And he has a good head for business. But best of all he's romantic," I said loudly, hoping the notion might rub off on Danny.

"Any idea who that might be?" Danny asked.

"Let me see the book again."

"Here." Danny held the book for me.

It fell open to the chapter on famous people. My eyes almost popped out. There was the name of the famed mystery writer, Leigh, written with an ornate flourish.

"Let me see that," I said, almost pulling the book out of Danny's hand. I held it close, studying the slant, the loops, the beginning and ending strokes. "This is so cool— the author Marty Leigh's handwriting."

"Who's Marty Leigh?" Danny asked.

"You don't *know?*"

He leaned back on the cement wall, crossing his arms in front of him. "Should I?"

"She's the greatest mystery writer of our time," I said proudly. But I didn't say that I was pen pals with her nephew, Lucas.

"*She?* So Marty must be a woman."

"And what a writer she is." I didn't like the way Danny

was looking at me. Like he doubted my opinion.

"Guess I'm not much into novels," he said.

"If you don't like fiction, what's left?" I studied him in-credulously.

"For me it's science and nature books, mostly."

"I like nature, too. But I also love fiction."

"Nonfiction broadens the mind. You should try it more often. It's true, you know. Fiction is merely someone's imagination running wild."

I wasn't sure where he was going with this. "I thought you were interested in my fiction . . . my imagination running wild," I reminded him.

"Sure, I'll read your stories sometime. Right now we have a mystery to solve."

"I'm not sure if we do or not," I said, feeling hurt.

"What's wrong, Holly?"

"There's only one mystery, and I'm looking at him," I said, dashing off down the sidewalk, my tablet and book under my arm, my backpack slung over one shoulder.

"Holly!" he called after me.

Danny had to know what I meant. Billy and Andie and everyone in Dressel Hills seemed to. I had every right to be upset.

I walked faster. "I know exactly who wrote the letter from Hawaii," I said. "I have to get home and tell my mom. See ya."

Then I took off running, leaving Danny-cold-fish-Myers behind without a clue.

I ran all the way home. Past the village ski shops and down the narrow street of my childhood. Away from Danny.

Carrie and Stephanie were sitting on the front-porch swing sipping lemonade. Their soft giggles mingled with the squeaky swing. When I reached them I was out of breath, but couldn't wait another second to ask Stephie the question burning inside me. "Did . . . your brothers . . . go to Japan?"

"Yes," she said.

"And . . . Hong Kong?"

"Yes," she repeated.

"What about Hawaii?" I asked, catching my breath.

"Last week," she said sheepishly.

"The night you were here for supper, right?"

Stephie nodded, her chin-length hair bouncing.

"The night Mr. Tate announced his plans to marry Mom?"

"Uh . . . yeah," she said, her brown eyes growing wide.

"You talked to your father on the phone long-distance

that night when you went back to the Millers' house, didn't you?"

Her lower lip trembled. "Uh-huh," she said in a squeaky get-set-for-tears voice.

I picked Stephie up off the porch swing, twirling her around and around, squealing, "Yes!"

We fell into a heap on the redwood floor of the porch, nearly knocking over the pots of Chinese-red geraniums. Mom poked her face out the door, obviously puzzled.

"Perfect," I said when I saw her. "You're just the person we need to talk to."

"Before you do, have you seen those silly letters anywhere?" she asked, holding the screen door open a few inches.

"Oh, those." I reached for my backpack. It had landed topsy-turvy under the porch swing. "Here." I handed them to her.

Her eyes narrowed. "Holly Meredith . . ."

"Before you get upset, Mom, I have some news that'll make your hair stand up and boogie."

Carrie and Stephie giggled, even though I was certain Stephie knew what I was about to announce.

"Here, Mom, you need to sit down first," I said, taking her arm and guiding her to a chair like she was a helpless invalid. I stood back and made a pretend drum roll in mid-air. "Are you ready for this?"

"Tell us!" Carrie shrieked.

"This announcement is all about true love," I said. "For . . . I am quite certain that Uncle Jack's in love with you, Mom."

Stephie and Carrie began jumping up and down, giggling.

"Please, girls," Mom said, insisting they sit down. "Now, Holly, what on earth are you saying?"

I began to unravel the tale of two letter writers. "One was a teenage boy who got the ball rolling as a practical joke with two anonymous letters to you, after overhearing a description of Mr. Tate's lack of hair."

"Bald Tate," said Stephie, no doubt repeating the term she'd used to her brother Stan on a long-distance phone call.

Mom looked completely lost as I unraveled the mystery. "Will you please slow down, Holly?"

"Okay," I said. "But think about it . . . remember the long-distance call I told you about? It must've been Stan disguising his voice, pretending to check up on the letter he'd mailed from Japan."

Mom leaned forward, listening more carefully.

"And after *that* phone call came the third letter, surprising us with new handwriting. . . . A different person. Another writer!"

"We *know* all this," Mom said, pushing a strand of blond hair away from her face.

"Yes, well, Stephie ate supper with us the night Mr. Tate told us his plan to move us to the mountains and start a bee farm," I said, eyeing Stephie. "Later that night, she talked to her father in Hawaii."

Mom looked disturbed. She started to speak. "Oh, Holly—"

"There's more," I interrupted. "The best part is this. What Stan started as a joke turned out to be a way for Uncle Jack to take up where Stan left off, with his beehive joke . . . and the 'sweet thoughts of you' sign-off. Stephie, tell my mom I'm not making this up."

"Well?" Mom said, leaning over to look into the freckled face of her sneaky little niece. "Did you play spy-kid at our house?"

"I leaked the info," she said in a tiny voice.

"You told your daddy about my plans with Mr. Tate?" Mom asked.

"Daddy said to tell him if you were dating anyone. *And* if you were happy. That's when I told him about the marriage license and the log cabin. And . . . you know, stuff like that."

"Why do you think your daddy wanted to know about these things?" Mom asked, holding the lemonade glass without drinking.

"Because nobody, except Carrie, was very happy about Mr. Tate. Especially you, Auntie Susan."

I watched Mom's expression. "Don't you see, Mom?" I said. "All of us knew it but you."

"Well," Mom said. "No sense fussing over the past."

"I agree," I said, tickling Stephie. "What else is Uncle Jack planning?"

"More secrets," Stephie said, giggling so hard she fell over.

I started to say, "Fab—"

"—ulous," Carrie finished for me. "Just fabulous!"

"Isn't this the most amazing and romantic thing?" I said.

"Don't jump to conclusions," Mom said, pouring lemonade for me. "It's just three silly letters."

"That's what *you* think," Stephie said and started giggling again. Her chestnut hair flew around her little head as she danced around the porch, almost bumping Mom's geraniums.

It was obvious Stephie knew more than she was telling. Much more! What *was* Uncle Jack up to . . . really?

16

Wed, August 25, I wrote in my journal. *My love life isn't even half as exciting as Mom's! I just found out that she and Mr. Tate ended things over the phone, and yesterday we found out that Uncle Jack is her secret admirer. Still, it's been the three longest days of my life—since Danny and I had our dumb fight. Should I call him or wait for him to make the next move?*

Closing my journal, I sat at my desk and stared out the window. Waiting for Danny could take forever . . . it could be Christmas before we got things worked out. *Worked out?* We weren't even really clicking at all.

Besides that, there was Kayla Miller—forever smiling at Danny, always sneaking around corners.

I sighed, slumping down on my window seat. Bearie-O flopped against me. Compared to Mom's relationships, my friendship with Danny was a joke.

Another letter showed up in the mailbox today . . . for *her!* Postmarked Seattle. I tried holding it up to the light in my room, but it was no use. I couldn't see through the envelope.

"I know who it's from," Stephie said, sneaking into my

bedroom and coming up behind me. "It's from my daddy!"

"Someone should teach you some manners," I said, hiding the letter behind my back. "Still spying, I see."

She rolled her eyes and zipped her lips shut, throwing away the "key."

When Mom arrived home, she snatched up the letter and disappeared into her bedroom like a squirrel hoarding a precious acorn. I wasn't surprised later when she said—with a twinkle in her eyes—that I would not be reading *this* one.

On Friday a dozen pink roses arrived for Mom before she got home from work. I sneaked a look at the card. It said: *From your not-so-secret admirer.* Now, here was a guy Danny Myers could take lessons from.

Then, to top things off, Uncle Jack called after supper.

"What's up?" I asked as Mom hung up the phone.

"Uncle Jack and the boys are back in town. He invited me to spend tomorrow evening with him," she said, acting like it was no big deal.

"And?"

"He said to dress very casually."

"Where's he taking you?"

"He was very secretive about it," Mom said, seeming to enjoy the mystery aspect most of all.

"So how casual is *very casual?*" I asked.

"I guess I'll have to investigate my wardrobe." She gave me a hug before dashing up the stairs.

"But this is your first date with Uncle Jack," I called to her. "Shouldn't you wear something wonderful?"

She shrugged it off. "Oh, you know your uncle," she said off-handedly. But her smile gave her away.

I took the phone downstairs to my "office" and called

Andie. "Mr. Tate and Mom really are through, just like I thought," I said. "It's so cool, and now my uncle's taking her out."

"You're kidding. Your *uncle* and your mom on a date? How weird is that?"

"They're *not* related," I said. "Not by blood, anyway."

"He was married to your dad's sister, right?"

"Uh-huh. Aunt Marla died six months ago."

"Speaking of guys and girls, how are things between you and Danny?" she asked.

"Not so good," I said. "Last Sunday, he started putting down the kind of books I like. I got fed up and told him off."

"You did? Whoa, Holly, that's not a good way to win friends and influence people."

"No kidding." I was beginning to feel sorry about the blowup.

"What about the older man in your life . . . uh, Lucas what's-his-face?" she asked.

"Lucas *Leigh*," I corrected her. "He owes me a letter, and I should be getting my story critique back from him soon." I didn't tell her about the cool picture I'd sent with my gloriously grown-up hairstyle.

"Better hope Danny doesn't find out about Lucas," she warned.

"*You're* the only one who knows about that, so . . ."

"My lips are sealed," she said. "Gotta run. Bye."

When I hung up, I heard giggling just outside my "office" door. I sneaked over, listening, then opened the door quickly. Carrie and Stephie ran screaming in opposite directions.

"What's with you two?" I demanded.

Carrie played the innocent while Stephie kept laughing, crouching behind the sectional.

"Don't you know it's rude to eavesdrop?" I said. "This better never happen again."

"Or what?" Carrie asked, eyes shining.

"Yeah." Stephie peeked over the sofa. "Or what?"

"That's it . . . I'm telling Mom," I said, stomping up the steps.

When I found her, Mom was in her room, staring blankly into her closet. Nope, she wasn't in the mood for tattling. "Solve things with your sister and cousin the best you can," she advised.

"But, Mom," I whined.

"This is Stephie's last night here," she said. "Can you endure the kid stuff till tomorrow at noon when Uncle Jack comes to pick her up?"

"Only if you can keep her and Carrie out of my life between now and then," I said, frustrated.

"Uh-huh," she muttered.

I could see she was too preoccupied with picking out just the right *very casual* outfit for her date with Uncle Jack.

Clumping off to my room, I complained to my journal instead. Mom and Uncle Jack were hot topics, of course. But more important was Lucas Leigh and his fabulous letters. I reread all of them.

Then, when the mail arrived the next day, I hit the jackpot. Three letters! One from my pen pal in Austria, one from Daddy in California, and one from Lucas Leigh. I sat on the porch and tore open Lucas's letter, reading it first.

Dear Holly,

Thanks for your recent letter and picture. I hope you don't mind that I passed your story "Love Times Two" on to my aunt, Marty Leigh. She has some comments to make about it, and she'd like to make them in person. She's scheduled to go on a book tour to promote her hot new kids' series, and—believe it or not—we'll be in Dressel Hills at the Explore Bookstore on Labor Day. Would you like to meet us there around 12:30 for lunch? If I don't hear differently from you, I'll assume it's a go.

My aunt wants to discuss with you the possibility of including "Love Times Two" in the first issue of a new teen magazine she is starting, called Sealed With a Kiss. *Interested?*

Looking forward to meeting you, Holly!

Lucas W. Leigh

P.S. I've enclosed a photo of myself you may keep.

I stared at the picture. Lucas Wadsworth Leigh was the best-looking college guy I'd seen in my entire life. Could it be he wanted to take me to lunch nine days from now . . . right here in Dressel Hills? And what was this about maybe becoming published?

My heart pounded as I scooped up the other letters and dashed inside the house to the phone. I punched Andie's number.

Br-ring! *Please be awake, Andie. I need you!*

Br-ring! It rang again.

"Hello?" Thank goodness she answered.

"Andie," I said. "I'm desperate for your expert help. Can you come right over?"

"What's going on?" she asked. "Is this about Danny?"

"Worse, er, better—oh, just get over here. I'll tell you then." We hung up.

On the way to my room, I brushed past Stephie and Carrie sitting on the stairs. "Watch it," Carrie said.

"Yeah," Stephie said, carrying her overnight bag down to the living room.

Good, I thought. *Stephie's leaving. One less snoop around here.*

Carefully closing my door, I wished there was a lock on it for private occasions. That wasn't all I wished. I wished I'd told the truth. I'd led Lucas to think I was much older.

I sat very still on my window seat, contemplating my dilemma. A very famous author, Marty Leigh, wanted to talk about publishing me in her new teen mag. Would she still want my story when she found out I was only thirteen and a half?

Leaning over, I brushed my long hair down, hoping to put it up the way Danny's mom had a week ago. Getting my hair into a French twist was the least of my worries. What kind of clothes would a woman wear to meet none other than Marty Leigh and her fabulous nephew—my gorgeous hunk of a pen pal—LWL?

I tore through my closet and found absolutely nothing.

17

"You told him what?" Andie said, plopping herself cross-legged on the floor in my bedroom.

"It's not *what* I said. Just what I *didn't* say," I moaned, sticking my head out my bedroom door and scanning the hall for kid-sized snoopers.

"You've gotta be warped right down to your split ends, Holly Meredith."

I leaped onto my bed. Andie just sat there on the floor, her eyes boring a hole in me. She was right. There was no easy way out of *this* mess.

"C'mon, Holly. You know you have to tell this babe Lucas the truth."

"You sound like *me* talking to *you*," I said, sorting through his letters for the zillionth time. I found the first letter Lucas W. Leigh had ever written to me. His penmanship was nearly as good as Danny's mother's. His A's and O's were carefully closed, meaning he could keep a secret.

Andie crawled over to the bed. "What're you doing?"

"Analyzing his handwriting."

"What for?"

"To see if he's accepting and . . ." I hesitated.

"And what?"

I sighed. "Forgiving."

Andie held Bearie-O close to her. "What's the big deal? Give the man a call and tell him the truth. If he's as smooth as you think, he'll laugh it off. If not, forget it."

"That's easy for you to say." I rolled over and propped myself up on my elbows. I told her about his aunt—my favorite author. "Think about it—Marty Leigh has plans for my story, 'Love Times Two.' "

"You mean *our* story," Andie said. "Remember it's about me, too."

I ignored her. "I made a wish, Andie. And it's starting to come true."

Her eyes bugged wide. "What wish?"

"It probably sounds stupid, but I made a wish on the last letter I sent Lucas," I said, remembering the magical moment.

"What sort of wish?"

I took a deep breath, eyeing my friend. "Don't laugh, please?"

"I promise."

"The wish was about writing to Lucas, hoping it might lead me to find the truth about my stories. If I have any writing talent."

"So you used him because of his author-aunt," she stated flatly.

"It's just that if I could somehow know I had true writing talent, I'd work day and night to write as well as Marty Leigh."

"That I'd like to see. Holly the Sleepless Author," she said, making fun.

"Anyway, if I blow things now and tell the truth about my age, maybe Leigh won't—"

"Won't want to mess with a kid writer," she interrupted me.

"Right. So . . . I have a plan. Will you help me?"

"Help you continue this charade?" She was twisting a dainty curl around her finger.

"Not really continue anything, just try to look as old as I did in the picture."

"*What* picture?"

"The drugstore picture I had taken after Danny's mom did my hair last Saturday," I explained.

Andie frowned. "Why don't you just call Mrs. Myers? I'll bet she'd be happy to help you look exactly the same way again."

It *wasn't* funny. "Don't you dare breathe a word of this to her or to—"

"I know, I know . . . to precious Danny," she said.

"Promise?"

"Maybe, maybe not."

"Andie! I won't introduce you to my cousin," I bribed her.

"Hmm, Stan's a real hunk. Sure wouldn't want to miss out on *that*," Andie said, scratching her head. "All right, worry-bean, you win."

I smiled. "Here's the plan. Can you get your hands on some *dark* mascara and eyeliner?"

"Mom's got tons of it," she said.

"Perfect. Make sure you get it over here by ten o'clock on Labor Day morning."

"Why so early? That's the last day to sleep in before school starts."

"C'mon, Andie, cooperate with me. You have all next week to sleep in."

"Yeah, yeah," she said, getting up to leave. "See you in church tomorrow." She turned around and giggled at me. "Can't believe you got yourself into such a mess, Holly. It's so hilarious."

"Get outta here," I said, tossing a heart-shaped pillow at her.

She caught the pillow and threw it back. "What I wouldn't give to tell Danny Myers about all this."

I leaped off the bed. "Andie, you promised!"

"Oh yeah, almost forgot."

I opened my bottom dresser drawer and ripped a page out of my journal. "Here," I said, shoving the paper under her nose. "Write your name."

"What for?" Her eyes were wide.

"Just do it."

She scribbled *Andrea Martinez* with a pen from my dresser.

"Thanks," I called after her as she dashed down the stairs.

"Happy analyzing," she yelled back.

I stared at the paper. Not a single A in her name was closed at the top!

I froze. If the handwriting book was true, Andie's open A's meant she could *not* keep a secret. Not at all.

♥　　♥　　♥

Uncle Jack showed up after lunch to pick up Stephie. His handsome face looked tan from his time in Hawaii, and his wavy brown hair had blond streaks from the sun.

"Daddy!" Stephanie called to him, running to the door.

"Hi, shortie," he said, gathering her up for a big bear hug. He leaned over and wrapped his arm around Carrie, too. Then he spotted me, hanging back close to the stairs. "Whatcha hiding over there for, Holly?"

He came over and gave me a big squeeze. How good he smelled—fresh, like summer wind.

"Take a look at this young lady," he said. "Boys must be calling 207 Downhill Court day and night."

I brushed my hair away from my shoulder. "Thanks," I said, blushing, as always.

Carrie jumped on his back, pulling the collar of his shirt. He grabbed her and swung her around. She squealed. "Where are you taking Mommy on a date?"

Uncle Jack lowered his voice mysteriously. "On a very special secret surprise."

"I wanna come, too," Carrie said.

"Me too. Me too," Stephie squealed.

"Well," Uncle Jack said, pulling his pretend beard, "if we take you along, what about Holly?"

"And Stan and Phil and Mark," shouted Carrie.

By now the girls had wrestled Uncle Jack to the floor. Mom appeared from the kitchen just as Stephie sat on his back. Carrie messed up his hair, giggling hysterically. It was good to see *hair* again.

Mom smiled, wiping her hands on a towel.

"Hello, Susan," Uncle Jack said, sitting up and pulling Stephie onto his lap while Carrie hung on his neck.

"Hi," Mom said, almost shyly. "Looks like you've met our welcoming committee."

"And some welcome it was," he said, tickling Carrie and Stephie again.

"We're going on a date with you, Mommy," Carrie announced, trying to pull Uncle Jack's Reeboks off.

"There's room for everyone," Uncle Jack said, looking at Mom. "But only if it's okay with my date." There was an irresistible twinkle in his voice.

"Sounds like fun," Mom said, laughing.

Uncle Jack jumped off the floor, bringing the girls up with him. "Okay, then, we'll see you ladies at five-thirty."

"Give us a hint where we're going," Carrie begged.

"Only one," he said, pulling a piece of straw out of his plaid shirt pocket and slipping it into his mouth. "What political office does a horse run for?" he asked, with the straw dangling off his lips.

"What's 'political'?" Carrie asked.

"I'll tell you later," Uncle Jack said, poking her ribs.

I stood close to Mom. "What political office *does* a horse run for?" I asked.

"Mare," Uncle Jack said, straight-faced.

For some reason, the joke struck me funny. I laughed till the tears came to my eyes.

"I don't get it. What's the hint?" asked Carrie.

"The joke's the clue," Uncle Jack said, kissing her forehead. "Think about it."

"Don't worry, Carrie. *I* don't get it, either," Stephie said, heading toward the door with her dad. Mom and I followed behind them.

"Jump in the van," Uncle Jack told Stephie, taking the straw out of his mouth and shoving it into his blue jeans.

Carrie hurried off to see our boy cousins while Mom and I stood on the porch, waving to them in the van. Stan sat smugly behind the wheel, waving his driving permit at me. Phil and Mark hung halfway out the windows.

Mom quietly thanked Uncle Jack for the roses.

"My pleasure," he said, giving her a peck on the cheek, the way he used to when all of us visited Uncle Jack and Aunt Marla back east.

He kissed me, too. "Wear your rattiest jeans tonight," he said with a wink.

Carrie raced back to the porch as the sleek gray van pulled out of the driveway and disappeared down our street.

I turned to Mom. "Where do *you* think we're going?"

"Think about it," she said, playing Uncle Jack's game.

"You *know*, don't you?" I said, glad to see the stress gone from her eyes.

"It'll be a date to remember," she said.

I ran upstairs to add important info to my journal, starting with Lucas and ending with Uncle Jack.

Soon it was time to get ready for the "family" date. It felt weird and good at the same time. I wondered if Lucas would ever want to invite *my* whole family on a date. Then I remembered it was just last week that *Danny* had suggested Mom and Carrie and I come to his house for dinner sometime. Like that would ever happen.

Carrie ran past my room shouting, "Look, there are horses in our street!"

I gave my hair a final brushing and flew down the steps to see.

A hay wagon, pulled by two horses, waited like Cinderella's pumpkin coach. Stan, Phil, and Mark sat in the back, chewing long pieces of straw. Uncle Jack jumped down off the wagon, heading for the house.

"Mom!" I called upstairs. "You're never gonna believe this."

"Believe what?" She appeared at the head of the stairs, a sweater draped over her shoulders.

I stared at her. "Mom, you look so young tonight."

"Why, thank you, Holly-Heart. I *feel* young," she said, fluffing her hair in the mirror just as the doorbell rang.

Funny, I thought. *Mom and I should trade places on Labor Day when Lucas Leigh comes to town.*

Mom went to the door and opened it. There stood Uncle Jack, grinning. "Are m' ladies ready?" he asked, tipping his straw hat.

"Certainly," Mom replied, taking his arm. They walked down the sidewalk, very dignified.

Carrie, my cousins, and I burst into loud giggles. *What a change from Mr. Tate*, I thought as I clambered aboard the wagon. *Thank you, Lord!*

18

Exactly one week later Uncle Jack took all of us out on a "date" again. Guess we made a good impression the first time. Anyway, it was fun having so many relatives around—even if it meant squeezing all of us into a single raft on the wild Arkansas River.

That night I wrote in my journal about riding the rapids with Uncle Jack and our cousins. No one fell overboard this time, but we *did* get soaked. Best of all, I couldn't remember seeing Mom laugh so much.

Counting the hours till I met Lucas face-to-face took most of my energy, as well as my thoughts. Andie and I did a practice run on my makeup and hair after church on Sunday. It was amazing the difference a little—*a lot*—of makeup could do. To complete the look, I found the perfect tailored suit at a secondhand shop.

But on the day of Lucas's visit, Andie showed up ten minutes late. She had me totally freaked by the time she arrived.

"Hey, it's Labor Day," she said. "What do you expect? My mom had me hand-washing and waxing the floors."

"Right," I said. "Somehow I can't picture it. But nice try anyway."

"Hold still," she insisted, carefully outlining my eyes with dark liner.

A whole hour and a half later, I was ready.

"Now what?" Andie stepped back, admiring her handiwork.

"Let's role-play till it's time for me to leave," I said.

"Huh?" Andie stared wide-eyed at me.

"You be Lucas, and I'll be me."

"You're crazy."

"Not really. It helps to plan what I'll say."

"You mean you don't know?" Andie said.

"I have a plan."

"Oh great," she muttered. "Another plan."

The phone rang. "For you, Holly," Mom called to me.

I whispered to Andie, "Check to see if my mom's downstairs."

She crept out into the hallway and peered down the staircase. "All clear."

I dashed to the hall phone, keeping my face toward the wall. "Hello?"

"Hi, Holly." It was Danny.

"Oh, hi," I said softly, hoping Mom would stay downstairs.

"I've missed you," he said.

"You have?" I said, wondering why he hadn't called for two whole weeks.

"Yeah," he said. "I know it's been a long time since we researched the handwriting book at the library, but . . ."

"Look, Danny," I said, checking my watch, "I'm really

sorry, but I can't talk now. I'm kinda in a hurry. Can we talk later?"

"Please listen. I'll make it short."

"Okay."

"I've been thinking," he said. "About us, er . . . you and me, you know."

"Uh-huh?" I heard footsteps on the stairs. My heart pounded. No way could I let Mom see me this way.

"Holly," Danny said, taking a deep breath. "Would you consider going with me?"

I saw the top of Mom's head out of the corner of my eye. She was coming upstairs fast.

"Uh, sorry, Danny, I'll have to talk to you later. Bye!" I left the phone dangling as I dashed to my bedroom and slammed the door. Hiding in the closet, I told Andie, "If Mom wants me, I'm unavailable."

"Are you crazy?" she said through the crack in the closet door. "What's going on?"

Just then . . . *knock, knock.*

"Holly, come hang up this phone, please," Mom said.

I heard Andie open my bedroom door. "I'll do it," she said, closing the door safely behind her.

Inside the dark closet, I suddenly felt disloyal to Danny in my globbed-on getup, preparing for a rendezvous with Lucas Leigh. All summer I'd waited for this moment—for Danny to ask this question—and now I couldn't even give him an answer! All because I was hiding from Mom. Still, I couldn't give up this game I was playing with Lucas. Or with myself.

♥　　♥　　♥

Once Andie was absolutely sure Mom was out of sight, I stuffed all my Leigh mysteries in an overnight case and sneaked down the stairs and out the back door.

Andie walked me to Aspen Street, where we said good-bye. She wished me luck with Lucas and made me promise to tell her every juicy detail.

Downtown, the souvenir shops bustled with end-of-summer tourists. I caught my reflection in the donut-shop window as I made my way to the Explore Bookstore. Pushing my shoulders back, I snickered at the shapely look I'd achieved with a wad of tissues stuffed in all the right places. No question, I *was* older than thirteen.

As I waited for the light to change, I heard Jared Wilkins' voice behind me. "Holly, is that you?"

I kept facing forward as I heard him running to catch up with me. I ignored the traffic light, hoping to lose Jared in the shuffle of cars and people.

"Wait, Holly! Watch out!" he shouted.

A car swerved. I kept running, raising my left hand to protect my perfect French twist. Only half a block more to the bookstore.

Just then, I felt a hand on my shoulder. Jared whirled me around. "You could've gotten yourself killed back there."

"What do you want?" I said, anger and embarrassment boiling up inside me.

He stepped back, a perplexed look on his handsome face. "Well, well, what is *this?*"

"None of your business, that's what. Now, leave me alone."

"You look absolutely dazzling, Miss Meredith," he said,

his eyes focusing on my hair. "I've never seen you look so, uh . . ."

"Grown-up?" I said.

He snapped his fingers. "That's it! You look much older. But why?"

"Please excuse me," I said, pushing past him.

"Going my way?" he asked.

"I hope not," I said, cringing inside. Jared would blow my cover for sure. It would serve me right for thinking I could pull off such deception.

"Man, Holly, you're acting so strange."

I looked at my watch. *Five minutes to go.* "Will you *please* get lost?" I asked, my voice shaking.

"Hey, don't cry," he said, backing away. "If it means that much to you, I'm outta here. See you at school tomorrow."

I stood there close to tears as my former heartthrob turned and walked away. Jared was right—I *was* acting strange. So strange I hardly recognized myself.

Dreadful apprehension—and a bit of determination— flared up inside me as I headed for the bookstore.

The place hummed with people, overflowing with quiet conversation and occasional laughter. Ferns and ivy hung in potted baskets from the ceiling. Bamboo chairs were scattered around for book-inspecting by prospective buyers.

Then I saw him . . . Lucas Leigh. Unmistakably, my summer pen pal.

Quickly, I hid in the corner, behind one of the high-backed bamboo chairs. There, I was able to observe him privately. Wearing navy blue dress pants and light blue dress shirt, he seemed older than his picture. And attentive to each of the fans waiting in line.

I felt really ridiculous hiding in this outrageous getup. Pulling a tiny mirror from my purse, I checked my makeup. The new Holly smiled back at me, French twist and all. Thoughts of honesty crept into my mind, spoiling the moment. I felt jittery. Even sinful.

I glanced at the wide table where Lucas stood beside a stack of Marty Leigh's most recent book. My favorite author wore a bright green two-piece dress with pearl earrings. She was signing a book for an obvious fan. The girl watched her, apparently awestruck.

Feeling as shy as the girl looked, I drew a deep breath and stood up. It was now or never.

I tried to move but stood frozen behind the chair. Then something inside me popped loose. The truth! It was time to let it emerge. I began pulling the pins out of my French twist on the way to the ladies' room. Inside, I searched for a brush in my purse and some tissues to wipe off the eye makeup.

"Please, Lord, forgive me," I whispered as I shook my hair free. Frantically, I washed away the heavy makeup. Next I pulled out the tissue wads, revealing my own true shape, such as it was.

Stepping back, I admired the real Holly Meredith in the mirror. Perfect.

Then, taking a deep breath, I left the rest room and marched toward Lucas Leigh and the book-signing event. I waited in line like the others, and when it was my turn at the book table, I said, "Hello, Lucas. I'm Holly Meredith."

He looked a bit surprised but shook my hand and held it while he introduced me to his aunt. "Marty, this is Holly, the writer of 'Love Times Two.'"

"So very pleased to meet you, Holly," she said, smiling broadly.

Gently, I pulled my hand away from Lucas and shook hands with Marty Leigh.

Lucas seemed confused. "I hardly recognized you, Holly. You looked much older in your picture," he said. "I thought—"

"I'm sorry," I confessed. "I must tell both of you the truth about myself. I'm really only thirteen and a half. I shouldn't have misled you. I guess I wanted to impress you."

Miss Leigh smiled warmly. "Holly, dear, you don't have to impress me. I'm already impressed with you."

"You are?" I felt self-conscious with Lucas staring at me.

"Oh yes," she said. "You have a marvelous talent, my dear. And thirteen or thirty, I plan to help you get published." She touched her single strand of pearls.

Lucas nodded, smiling. "I hope you can join us for lunch, Holly."

"I'd like that," I said, surprised at his reaction to the real me. The line of people was growing longer behind me. I reached for my overnight case, filled with many Leigh mysteries. "I'd be honored if you'd sign these," I said.

She wrote her name in each book, just as it had appeared in the handwriting book Danny and I discovered at the library. When she finished, I thanked her generously. Then Lucas escorted me upstairs to the coffee shop while my favorite author of all time continued to sign books and greet her adoring fans.

"My aunt will join us soon," Lucas said, leading me to a table near the windows. "How's this?"

"Fine, thanks," I said as he pulled out the chair for me.

"You certainly don't write like a thirteen-year-old," he said, handing the menu to me. "Your story was better than most of the stories my college classmates write."

"Thanks." I blushed, which was probably a good thing, after scrubbing all that makeup off. About now, I could use a little color on my face.

"It's true," he said, reading the menu. "Please, order whatever you'd like."

"How about a cheeseburger with everything on it?"

"Just what my younger sister usually orders."

"Really? You never mentioned her in your letters," I said, realizing how dumb my comment was, especially since a considerable amount of info had been missing from *my* letters, as well.

"How old is she?" I asked.

"Almost thirteen, and she loves to write. Especially letters."

"Think she'd want a pen pal?"

"Good idea," he said, smiling.

Soon Marty Leigh joined us, presenting a copy of her latest book to me. She ordered ginger ale for us, then proposed a toast. "Here's to *Sealed With a Kiss*." She raised her glass. "To the first issue."

In great detail, she explained her plan to include my short story in the November issue of the magazine.

"Are you willing to do some rewriting?" she asked.

"Whatever it takes." I felt giddy.

"That's the spirit," she said, taking another sip. "What do you think of the magazine title?"

"It's perfect," I said, pushing my hair back and letting it hang down behind my chair. I felt so good about going through with the truth. Maybe I'd write a book about this crazy day. Someday. For now, I'd have to record every amazing facet in my journal.

♥ ♥ ♥

That evening, I told Mom all about my thrilling day, especially the part about the new magazine.

"*Sealed With a Kiss* will be out in three months," I told her. "I can't wait to see my story in print."

"Our Holly-Heart is going to be a published writer," she said, reaching for my hands and dancing around the kitchen with me.

"How much money will you get for it?" Carrie asked.

"Wait and see." I laughed as Goofey arched his kitty back and meowed under the desk.

When all the hoopla died down, I excused myself and slipped off to my bedroom. What an incredible day this had been. In more ways than one!

Perched on my beloved window seat, I listened to my heart. And I wrote my answer to Danny Myers' important question.

About the Author

Beverly Lewis was struck with pen pal fever as a fourth grader. She continues to write letters (both snail mail and email), answering her readers from as far away as Ethiopia, Australia, and Scotland.

Writing cheery letters and notes to encourage family and friends has always been one of Beverly's favorite things to do. She keeps track of special days in a pocket-sized calendar.

Beekeeping? She's never done that, but her young friend Kimi Gariepy—who lives in Missouri—does, and told her all about it.

A former schoolteacher, Beverly enjoys creating newsletters to send via snail mail, as well as updating her Web site at *BeverlyLewis.com*. Check it out!

Also by Beverly Lewis

The Beverly Lewis Amish Heritage Cookbook

PICTURE BOOKS

Cows in the House   Annika's Secret Wish
Just Like Mama

THE CUL-DE-SAC KIDS
Children's Fiction

The Double Dabble Surprise	*Tarantula Toes*
The Chicken Pox Panic	*Green Gravy*
The Crazy Christmas Angel Mystery	*Backyard Bandit Mystery*
No Grown-ups Allowed	*Tree House Trouble*
Frog Power	*The Creepy Sleep-Over*
The Mystery of Case D. Luc	*The Great TV Turn-Off*
The Stinky Sneakers Mystery	*Piggy Party*
Pickle Pizza	*The Granny Game*
Mailbox Mania	*Mystery Mutt*
The Mudhole Mystery	*Big Bad Beans*
Fiddlesticks	*The Upside-Down Day*
The Crabby Cat Caper	*The Midnight Mystery*

ABRAM'S DAUGHTERS
Adult Fiction

The Covenant   The Sacrifice
The Betrayal   The Prodigal
The Revelation

THE HERITAGE OF LANCASTER COUNTY
Adult Fiction

The Shunning   The Confession
The Reckoning

OTHER ADULT FICTION

The Postcard • The Crossroad

The Redemption of Sarah Cain

October Song

Sanctuary* • The Sunroom

www.BeverlyLewis.com

*with David Lewis